TROUBLE WITH THE CEO

IONA ROSE

AUHOR'S NOTE

Hey there!

Thank you for choosing my book. I sure hope that you love it. I'd hate to part ways once you're done though. So how about we stay in touch?

My newsletter is a great way to discover more about me and my books. Where you'll find frequent exclusive giveaways, sneak previews of new releases and be first to see new cover reveals.

And as a HUGE thank you for joining, you'll receive a FREE book on me!

With love,

Iona

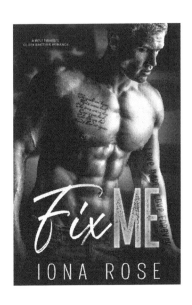

Get Your FREE Book Here:
https://dl.bookfunnel.com/v9yit8b3f7

Trouble With The CEO

Publisher: Some Books
ISBN- 978-1-913990-31-2

AVA

"Shots, shots, shots, shots," Sophie chants, looking down at the shots before looking up at me expectantly, a massive grin on her face that says she knows I'm going to protest, but that she also knows she'll be able to wear me down.

I glance down at the tray loaded with Sambuca shots in a range of colors that span the rainbow. I groan and shake my head. She's not going to be able to wear me down this time. I can't drink another shot. Even the thought makes me want to retch.

"No more for me," I say, holding my hands up and shaking my head vigorously. "I'm done here."

"Oh, come on Ava, don't be boring. We're meant to be celebrating graduating from college," Melanie adds, pushing one of the shots towards me with great determination.

I watch it slide towards me with a look of horror.

Melanie just laughs and keeps pushing the glass.

"Drink it, or it'll spill and what a waste that will be," she chants.

I shake my head.

"This is a once in a lifetime celebration," she cajoles.

"Do you want me to be sick?"

"You're not going to be sick. Anyway, it's not a celebration if you don't wake up with a hangover."

I stare at her.

"Come on. Don't let me get drunk on my own." She pushes her lip out like a pouty child. "Please, Ava, please."

"Ok, Ok," I laugh, holding my hands up in mock surrender.

Melanie stops pushing the little glass but her hand hovers around, ready to start up again if I back out now.

"But I swear this one is my last one."

I know I should have stood my ground, but Melanie is right. We're meant to be celebrating and it's not like we graduate from college every day. Ah fuck it. I'm only going to do this once so I may as well make it a good one I tell myself.

"Sure, that's your last shot," Sophie agrees with a wink that says 'until the next one'. "Now drink up."

I shake my head and roll my eyes, but I can't help but smile as I pick my shot up and down it. It burns my throat as I swallow it and my mouth floods with saliva at the aniseed taste. It's mixed with banana flavor, not a good combination in any way, and the taste of the aniseed mingled in with the fake sweetness of the banana makes me want to retch once more, and I quickly swallow a mouthful of my gin and tonic to wash away the taste. Sophie and Melanie look as though they enjoyed their shots about as much as I did.

"Remind me again why we drink these things when none of us actually like them," I ask, still grimacing from the sickly taste of the shot.

"Because they hit the spot." Melanie laughs, rubbing her belly.

I laugh with her. She kind of has a point. Once I get past the urge to retch, the warm feeling spreading through me is kind of nice. I'm already floating on air after graduating from college and the shots only make me feel even more giddy, even more happy.

Sophie grins at me and holds out another shot to me. I shake my head but Sophie makes no effort to take the shot away.

"Two for you because you're celebrating two things," she says. "Graduating and getting the job you wanted."

"It's kind of the same thing really," I say. "I already had the job offer dependent on me graduating."

"Irrelevant. You still need to celebrate," Sophie insists.

The last few shots must be doing their job because I no longer want to be sensible and refuse to drink the shot. Instead, I reach out, take it from Sophie and down it in one gulp. I chase it down with a gulp of gin and tonic, then stand up.

"Come on girls, let's hit the dance floor," I shout above the music. "I love this freaking song."

We make our way across the club, pushing our way through the warm and writhing bodies until we find a space on the dance floor. Then we begin to move. The combination of the heat, the alcohol and the thrumming of the music makes me feel wild and untamed, like I can really let my hair down tonight and just have fun.

As the three of us dance and drink, I realize that I don't want this night to end. It feels good to have this one weekend where I'm no longer a student and I'm not starting work until Monday. It's one last weekend of freedom where nothing defines me and I'm free to do whatever the hell I like. No studying to do, no assignments, no panicking about exams, and no work over the weekend. I love that. Even knowing it won't last forever doesn't make me sad like it perhaps should. In fact, I think knowing that it can't last forever is part of what makes it so special.

As I down the last of my drink, I'm aware I'm more than a little bit tipsy now. But I don't care. It's not like I'm falling down drunk. Not yet anyway. I'm just at that pleasant stage of drunk where everything is funny, and all of my inhibitions are starting to fall away. It's also that level of drunk where I know if I stop drinking now, it will wear off quickly and I won't be able to get it back. With that thought in mind, I stop dancing.

"Are you ok?" Sophie yells over the music, looking at me with a frown of concern as I look for a way through the throng of bodies on the dance floor.

"Yeah," I shout. "I'm fine. Better than fine. Great in fact. I'm just going to the bar. Same again?"

Sophie and Melanie both nod and keep dancing and I finally spot a small opening in the crowd and I make my way through it to the bar. I order our drinks – another gin and tonic for me and two vodka and Cokes for Melanie and Sophie - and then I take a moment to have a look around the club. The club is busy – busier than it was when we moved onto the dance floor - but it's not packed to the point where you can't move or where you can't get a drink without waiting for twenty minutes.

I get our drinks and pay for them and make my way back to Sophie and Melanie, somehow making it across the dance floor without spilling a drop. I hand the girls their drinks and start dancing again, taking a long drink of my gin and tonic. I kind of miss the burning heat of the shots and I wonder absently if I should have gotten more of them. No, I think that would have been a bad idea.

"Isn't that Darlene over there?" Melanie asks.

I look over at the area she's pointing to and I see that it is indeed Darlene. Great. Just the person I don't want to see tonight. Or any night really. It's not so much that Darlene and I are enemies, or even that we don't like each other as such, it's just that we're not each other's cup of tea. We're total opposites to each other and not in a good way.

I generally tend to be fairly quiet, and Darlene is pretty much the life of the party, and where I'm happy to be a part of the group, Darlene has to always be the center of attention. I find her particular brand of obsessive attention seeking annoying and she probably finds me boring. She's kind of treated her time at college as one long, four-year party and tonight, on the night to end it all, it's no surprise that she's dressed to kill.

In a skin tight red body con dress and heels so high it would give me vertigo. If she were to fall, I would be surprised if she doesn't break her ankle. Still it probably wouldn't faze her – after all, it would get her some more attention.

I catch myself being mean and I tell myself to stop it. It's likely the last time I'll have to see her, and the last time she will make me feel boring and inferior. Ok, so there's a bit of truth. I always feel like Darlene is looking down at me – boring plain little Ava - and that when she does it, other people follow her lead.

"Hi girls," Darlene calls, waving manically as she spots us.

She starts making her way over to us, smiling as though we're all best friends. She must be drunk I think to myself, or she would know that she thinks I'm not up to her class. She reaches us, making walking in her skyscraper shoes look easy. She grabs me by my upper arms, and quickly air kisses each of my cheeks. Wow I really must have drunk too much because I feel quite shell-shocked when she releases me. She moves on to Sophie and Melanie. At least they saw what was coming and had a moment to prepare themselves.

"It's so good to see you all," she trills, her voice, as always, just a little bit too loud and that's saying something in a club. "I was so worried I wouldn't get to say goodbye to you all. I mean I know we were hardly best friends, but four years is a long time to be around the same people, isn't it, and I reckon we'll all miss each other in our own little ways."

I would argue the point. I don't think I'll miss Darlene for one minute but I have to admit she makes a fair point about the people around us becoming familiar, and her sentiment is nicer than I would ever have given her credit for. I nod and smile.

"Yeah. It was nice meeting you Darlene," I say.

"You too honey," she replies with a flash of her Hollywood white teeth.

She clearly doesn't know my name and normally the fake show of friendship would annoy me, but tonight I let it wash over me. So what if she doesn't know my name? I only know hers because she's such a drama queen. I can't exactly judge her for not making the time to get to know anything about me.

She starts talking just loud enough to catch the attention of the people around us, laughing even louder than that. People are glancing over, some in amusement, some rolling their eyes. And of course, a lot drooling over her. I can feel my face burning as the attention focuses on our little group and I have to admit I'm more than relieved when Darlene moves on to the next unsuspecting group who she greets initially with a loud shriek across the club and a wave.

"You know," Sophie laughs when Darlene is out of ear shot. "I can never decide if I want to be more like Darlene, or if I want to strive to be the opposite of her as much as I possibly can."

I kind of know what she means and I nod and laugh. For all Darlene is annoying at times, there is no denying that she always seems to be having fun and she always has a gaggle of interesting people around her. I think it would be nice to be so unashamedly who I am and have that confidence.

"I'd settle for being able to walk in shoes like that," Melanie puts in, getting back enthusiastic nods from both Sophie and me.

We go back to dancing and I soon realize my drink is empty once more. I wiggle my glass in the air.

"Whose round is it?" I ask.

"Yours," both Sophie and Melanie say together.

They look at each other and laugh and I shake my head.

"I got these," I remind them.

"Yeah, but some of us have tuition to pay," Sophie grins.

"Not to mention rent, food, bills, bills and more stupid bills to pay," Melanie adds. "Oh, and did I mention paying bills?"

"I have bills to pay," I remind her with a laugh. "And rent to cover. And believe it or not, no one gives me free food either."

"Well yeah, but you have a job that covers all of that stuff easily," Sophie says. "There's no way waiting tables, or working in a store, or something covers it all. That's why we all have a shit ton of student debt and you don't."

I suppose she has a point there. Mr. Kramer, my employer at Kramer and Foley, the law firm I work at, paid for me to go to college and get a degree as a legal assistant. While I was a student, I worked part time but he still paid me my full salary, telling me that getting the degree was essentially part of the job.

I work as Mr. Kramer's legal secretary. I started as a general secretary when I left school and after a few months, Mr. Kramer asked me to be his personal secretary when his old one retired. After two years, he decided that he needed someone who understood the legal system a whole lot more than I did. I remember when he called me into his office and told me that. I thought I was being fired and I was so upset it took me a while to register the fact that not only was he not firing me, but the offer he was making me was more than I ever could have dreamed was possible.

I think now of my gorgeous uptown apartment that no student would ever be able to afford and my almost new, not cheap car, and I decide that yes, I can get another round in. I grin at the girls.

"Fine," I say, holding my hands up in surrender. "Same again?"

They both nod and I head back to the bar. The club is picking up now and the crowd is a little bit thicker but it's still not so bad that it's a tight squeeze at the bar. I order our drinks and pay for them. As I walk away from the bar, I spot Darlene again. She's heading towards the exit of the club with a guy hanging off her arm and most likely hanging on her every word while he's about it.

As they reach the door, she turns back to wave to someone and he turns around too and I see his face. He's damned hot. Darlene is clearly going home with him tonight. For the first time in my life I feel a pang of jealousy go through me at the thought of the night she is going to have. Horrified with myself I look away from them quickly and catch the eye of the waitress who is patrolling around the club selling shots from a tray. She raises the tray and an eyebrow in question and I nod my answer.

I move to the side slightly and put my drinks down on an empty table and fish some money out of my purse.

"Two please," I say.

"Seven dollars," the shot girl says.

I pay her and I'm rewarded with two electric blue shots. I shrug and pick up the first one and down it. The second one follows soon after it. It's slightly better than the Sambuca shots, but not by much. As I pick up our drinks and then start to head back to the dance floor again, I know that Darlene had the right idea getting out of here with her hottie in tow. And at this moment, I know I'm going to do the same thing tonight.

I'm going to embrace my inner Darlene and have a fun night with a guy I have known for all of ten minutes and I'm going to enjoy it. I'm going to let my hair down and have wild sex, the kind of sex I've only ever dreamed of having. But I'm going to do one thing better than Darlene. The guy I go home with is going to be even hotter than hers. I smile to myself. Yes, that sounds like a damned good plan, even if I do say so myself.

I rejoin the girls and by the time we finish our drinks and get some more, I've not forgotten my plan exactly, but I have convinced myself I was just being silly, just being drunk so to speak. I am no Darlene, nor do I want to be anything like her.

Still when I look up and spot the most handsome man I have ever seen in my life across the crowded room, I feel a stirring inside of myself, like my inner Darlene is waking up and giving me confidence.

"Go get him," she seems to say. "God Ava, have one night where you just act your age and have fun."

That voice makes it sound so easy, and suddenly I see that it is that easy. I just need to act like I'm confident and the hot guy won't know that it's all an act. How could he? He doesn't know anything about me. I can be anyone I want to be while I'm with him.

Suddenly the hot guy looks over towards me and for a split second, everything else fades away. I can't hear the pounding music anymore. I can't see the other people around me. All I can see is him.

And my God is he a sight to behold.

He's tall, a little bit over six feet I'd guess, and he has the sort of build that says he works out, but that he's not obsessed with building huge muscles. His dark brown hair is just long enough to hang in his eyes or get tossed about in the wind. He runs his fingers through it as he looks at me.

I can feel my body responding to him as surely as if he was right by my side, touching me. Goosebumps skitter back and forth across my skin and my clit tingles, my pussy damp-ening and longing to be filled by the handsome stranger.

The spell is broken when Sophie touches my shoulder. I half jump and look towards her. She frowns slightly.

"Are you ok?" she asks.

"Yeah, I'm fine. I was just lost in thought for a minute there," I say.

"Melanie needs to get out of here," Sophie says, nodding her head towards Melanie who stands beside her swaying wildly.

The drink seems to have hit Melanie all of a sudden and I think it's only Sophie's arm around her waist that's keeping her from falling over.

"I'm going to take her outside and grab a cab. Are you coming?" Sophie asks.

I start to nod, but I imagine the handsome stranger. I imagine that I can feel his warm lips on mine, his hands roaming over my body, and suddenly I'm shaking my head.

"No. If you don't mind, I think I'm going to hang around and grab another drink or two," I say.

"Are you sure?" Sophie says, looking around herself dubiously as if she suddenly expects a group of armed ninjas to appear or something. "You want to stay here on your own?"

"A couple of old school friends are here. I promised I'd go and grab a drink and catch up with them," I lie.

I don't know why I'm lying. I could tell Sophie the truth, but something stops me and I don't question it, I just roll with it. This way will definitely invite less questions and I reckon that's a good thing.

"Well if you're definitely sure you'll be ok," Sophie says, her voice trailing off.

I am definitely sure I'll be ok, hell I'll be better than just ok if I get my way tonight, but Sophie is sounding less and less sure of the idea of me staying behind here alone by the minute. I'm almost pleased when Melanie groans. She rubs her stomach with one hand and presses the other one to her mouth.

"Soph? I think I'm going to be sick," she says.

"Go," I tell Sophie who says a quick goodbye and starts to lead a very unsteady on her feet Melanie towards the exit.

They get through it without Melanie being sick which is a good thing. I feel kind of relieved once they're gone. I don't think I would have found the confidence to approach the handsome stranger with Melanie and Sophie watching me. But now there is nothing to stop me. If he rejects me, no one ever needs to know, so I have nothing to lose. But even as I think it, I know he won't reject me.

I know he should – he's at least three or four levels too hot for me – but I know he won't. I could see my own desire mirrored in his grey blue eyes when he looked at me. And I know it's only a matter of time before I am in his bed tonight.

CHRISTIAN

To say I'm not into clubbing would be an understatement. There was a time when I quite enjoyed it, when I was in my early twenties, but now, at thirty-one, I'm kind of over it. Yet here I am, standing in a club, the music pounding through me and the beer warming my insides nicely.

I usually can't stand the fact that the music is so loud that to talk to anyone you practically have to yell into their ear, but tonight, I'm glad for the thumping sound of the bass going through me. It penetrates my brain and stops me from thinking. Because if I let myself think too much, all I'm going to think about is the bad day I've had.

No. I won't go there.

One lost deal is nothing. I'll claw it all back next month or even next week. I say goodbye to the deal. Tonight I'll just keep the thumping sound in my mind, and if I really need to think, I'll think about that gorgeous red head I'm taking home tonight. She's a far better distraction than any music could ever be no matter how loud the DJ turns it up.

It was an accident that I spotted the gorgeous red head really. The club isn't exactly packed, but it's pretty full. Full enough that scanning your eyes around the room shouldn't be enough to really notice any one person over the others. But I noticed her alright.

It was her hair I noticed first – fire engine red, stick straight, and long enough to skim the tops of her breasts and draw the eye to them. It's the sort of hair that looks tacky on some girls, but not on this girl. On her it looks amazing, like she'd been born to wear that color.

As I had watched her, she'd looked up and our eyes had met for a moment. It felt like we communicated without words at this moment, like she was telling me to take her home tonight. I felt aroused just looking at her and my cock ached to feel her tight little pussy wrapped around it.

I could have approached her then, asked her if she wanted a drink… or more. And I know she would have said yes to either. I could see it in her eyes, eyes that told me I was hers tonight. Sparkling, confident eyes. I thought about going over to her, but I couldn't take my eyes off her for long enough to make a move. I just wanted to keep staring at her, drinking her in. I could have sat there like that all night, but then one of the other girls with her touched her arm and spoke to her and she looked away and the spell was broken.

Only at that moment though. I know that neither of us will be leaving this club alone tonight. Maybe it would be more accurate to say the spell was paused for a moment or two.

I go to the bar and order a Jack Daniels and Coke which I pay for and then I return to the place I was before. If the hot girl comes looking for me, that's where she'll look and I'd hate for us to accidentally miss each other. I don't know why I'm saying if she comes looking for me. I've never been more sure of anything in my life than I am about her. The way she looked at me was like she was already stripping me naked, already throwing me onto my back and straddling me. Yes, it's not if she comes looking for me. It's more when she comes looking for me.

I'm almost finished with my drink when I feel eyes on me. Instantly my skin tingles as though electricity is buzzing over me. I know without looking up that it's her, but I look up anyway. How can I not look up? How can I not want to look into those wonderful, pale green eyes again and lose myself in them once more?

I look up and of course I'm right and it is her. And she's not just watching me this time. No, this time, she's walking towards me, her stride long and purposeful, her hips swaying seductively with each step. She is watching me and as I glance up and meet her eyes, she smiles briefly, more a curling of the corners of her lips than anything. She looks down, runs her tongue over her bottom lip and then looks back up at me. I can hardly tear my eyes away from the glistening moisture her tongue leaves behind on her bottom lip. I ache to taste her, to hold her, to fuck her senseless.

I smile at her as she reaches me. She stops in front of me, looking up at me. I can't help but look down at her chest where her breasts move slightly with each breath she takes, her dress showing just the right amount of cleavage to be attractive while still being classy.

I look back up to her eyes - a sure sign of how gorgeous she is that my gaze is so easily drawn away from her body back to her eyes - and I bring my glass to my lips and drain the last of my drink, looking at her over the rim of the glass. I swallow and put the glass down, all without breaking eye contact with the gorgeous woman.

"Ready to leave?" I ask.

It works. The beauty smiles at me, a smile that shows me straight white teeth that look real rather than bleached. Her eyes twinkle when she smiles. She gives me a single nod of her head and then she reaches out and takes my hand in hers. Sparks fly through my hand and up my arm where her palm presses against mine and judging by the sharp intake of breath from the woman, she feels it too.

She turns away from me and heads back the way she came, her hand still in mind, leading me. I don't resist her; I'm only too happy to follow her, wherever she may be taking me. She leads me through the club and to the exit. We step outside and our breaths plume in front of us, white steam floating on the night air. If it's cold though, I don't feel it, and it seems the woman doesn't either, despite being dressed only in a short black dress.

She keeps leading me, taking me to the end of the building and around the corner towards the line of cabs. We don't get that far. As soon as we're out of sight of the door of the club, she stops walking and pushes me back against the wall. She leans into me and her lips brush across mine, leaving me feeling breathless and so turned on I think I might burst.

She moans as she runs her lips over mine again and I know she's feeling this crazy attraction every bit as much as I am.

She presses herself against my body, her lips locking onto mine. She is no longer teasing me. She's kissing me hungrily and I kiss her back, my hunger equal to hers. I run my hands down her back and cup her ass cheeks, pressing her body against mine.

She tastes of fruit and alcohol, but beneath that there is something else, something I can't place but that makes me want to devour her. It's an almost earthy taste, something primal. My hands move off her ass, roaming over her body. She writhes against me, her hands in my hair as she kisses me deeper and deeper, not even coming up for air.

As suddenly as she started kissing me, she stops, pulling away from me so abruptly that for a moment I think I must have hurt her. Her lips curl into that cat like half smile again and I relax. She's not hurt; she's just a tease.

"So, are you getting us a cab then or are you going to make us walk?" she purrs.

I grin at her, what I hope is a seductive grin but I think is more likely to be a goofy grin judging by how giddy I feel. I put my hand on the small of her back and guide her towards the line of cabs all sitting waiting for a fare.

"I'm Christian by the way," I say as we reach the first cab at the front of the line and I pull the door open and gesture for her to get in.

She flashes me a sexy smile as she ducks down to slip into the back of the cab.

"I'm Ava," she says.

Ava. It suits her. It's exotic yet strangely familiar, just like her. I get in the cab next to Ava. She hasn't moved all the way across the seat and I can feel her thigh against mine, her arm against mine, and I'm glad the journey to my place isn't too long. I don't think I could last too long without pouncing on delicious Ava and fucking her senseless right here in the back of the cab.

AVA

Even though I approached Christian with confidence, knowing deep down he wouldn't reject me, I'm still finding it kind of hard to believe that someone as hot as him is taking me back to his place. I mean I'm not ugly or anything, but I can imagine Christian dating models and Miss World types, not normal girls like me.

No matter how unbelievable it is though, I have no choice but to believe it because I'm here with him right now. I'm sitting so close to Christian in the back of the cab, I can almost smell the lust on him. Heat comes off his body in waves, wrapping itself around me and making me feel dizzy in a delicious sort of a way.

We haven't been in the cab for long, but already I can see the houses getting bigger and more expensive looking, the neighborhoods more exclusive. So Christian obviously has a good job then. I almost ask him what he does but I don't want to ruin the spark between us with mundane conversation like that. I wonder briefly if he might be a model or an actor but I tell myself that's unlikely. Even if I didn't recognize him, people at the club would have. He would have had a crowd all around him.

A couple of minutes later, the cab pulls up in front of a nice, decent sized house. Christian hands the cab driver a fifty dollar bill and tells him to keep the change and then we get out of the cab. I don't have much time to take in the house as he ushers me along the path and up the porch steps. He unlocks the door and stands back, gesturing for me to go ahead. I step into the darkened hallway and move to one side so Christian can follow me in.

He kicks the door closed behind himself and then he takes my hand and leads me up a wooden staircase, down a short hallway and into a room. His bedroom. A shiver of anticipation goes down my spine as I stand inside of Christian's bedroom. He turns and leans over my shoulder to push the door closed. His arm brushes against my shoulder and that's all it takes for the spark that's been threatening to ignite inside of me ever since I first laid on Christian to become an explosion.

Christian must feel it too because his mouth is suddenly on mine, his kiss hungry and passionate. His tongue pushes between my lips, finding my tongue and caressing it roughly. I kiss him back with as much enthusiasm as he is showing me. I let my purse drop to the ground, not even thinking about the fact that my cell phone is in there, and I put my arms around him, my hands moving up and down his back. I slip one hand up inside of his shirt and as my hand touches his skin, I feel him take a sharp intake of breath and it's all I can do not to grin.

His hands skim over my hips and up my sides and then back down them again. Christian grabs the bottom of my dress and we pull apart for a moment, long enough for me to raise my arms and him to pull my dress over my head and throw it somewhere behind him.

We come back together and I start to unbutton his shirt, my hands shaking slightly as I go, a mixture of lust and excitement about what's coming next. I finally get all of the buttons open and I push the shirt down Christian's arms without stopping kissing him. I press myself against him, feeling his skin against mine. His chest moves against mine, rubbing the lace of my bra over my nipples and making them harden instantly. They tingle and I moan softly and press myself harder against Christian's body, trying to get some relief from the scratchy, delicious torture of my bra.

Christian's hands roam over my back and he unhooks my bra almost as though he knows how much it's bothering me, and I step back slightly, letting the offending bra fall to the ground. Christian kicks it away as I move back closer to him again, my hands fumbling his jeans open. He puts one hand on the small of my back and his other hand moves to my breast, kneading it and then teasing the nipple with his fingers. I moan again and I push his jeans down.

He steps out of his shoes, kicking them away, and then his jeans follow. He quickly lifts up one foot and then the other, peeling away his socks, and we stand there for a moment, kissing breathlessly, both of us in our underwear and me in my heels.

Christian's hands roam over me and he runs his fingernails lightly down my sides sending delicious shivers through me. He hooks his fingers into the waistband of my panties at either side and pushes them down. They slide over my thighs and then drop to the ground. I step out of my shoes and slip the panties over my feet and then I kick them away from me. I don't see where they go. I don't care where they go.

Christian moves his mouth from mine and kisses down my neck and down my chest. He sucks one of my breasts into his mouth and flicks his tongue back and forth across my nipple, making me throw my head back and moan as tingles spread down through my body. I can feel my pussy getting wetter by the moment and I can hardly wait to feel Christian fill me up.

I feel as though he's read my mind when he releases my breast from his mouth and kisses back up my neck and then looking me in the eye, he begins to walk me backwards towards his bed. The cool night air feels icy cold against my still wet nipple but I know the heat off Christian's body will soon warm it back through again.

He turns me slightly and I frown as he moves me past the bed. He smiles at my confusion and before I can say anything, he stops walking me and turns me around, pulling me back against his body. I am standing with my back to his chest, his arms wrapped around my middle, and in front of us is a full length mirror. My breath catches in my throat as I look at us standing there in front of it. Desire thrums through me as I watch Christian's hand move down my body.

He runs his tongue up the side of my neck at the same time as he slips his fingers between my lips and finds my clit. He works me with an expert touch, making my already swollen clit pulse in time with my racing heart beat. He blows gently on my neck, turning the skin cold where he has just licked me. I make an "ah" sound as Christian increases the pressure on my clit and moves his fingers faster and faster. I can feel myself hurtling towards my climax, my pussy tingling and clenching in anticipation of what is to come.

Christian moves his other hand up my body, squeezing my nipple and sending a flash of delicious pain through me. The feeling from my nipple is intense, amazing, and it seems to collide with the feeling from my clit somewhere in the middle of my stomach, sending pleasure coasting through my whole body and taking my breath away.

I can't quite take my eyes off myself in the mirror. I've never done anything like this before. I'd have said I was too shy normally, but Christian seems to be bringing this adventurous side out of me. My skin is glowing with a sheen of sweat that makes it look as though my body has been dipped in glitter where the moonlight catches it. My face is flushed and my lips look dark red and swollen. My eyes have taken on a glassy look, the look of lust. I recognize it from looking into Christian's eyes and seeing it there.

I look down and watch Christian's hand as his fingers work my clit, bringing me closer and closer to the edge. There is something sensual about the way his hand moves, something almost graceful to the movement and it brings another rush of pleasure over me watching him moving within my lips like that.

Christian moves his hand from my breast and brings it to rest on my stomach and then he ups the pace of his fingers on my clit once more, working me until I'm gasping for breath and then, just when I think I can't take it anymore, he presses down on me, bringing my climax on in a rush.

I feel my pussy clench tightly, the muscles in my stomach tightening deliciously and I feel my whole body spring to life.

I rest my head back against Christian's shoulder, my eyes closed as I coast through wave after wave of pleasure. Even as my orgasm slams through me and my juices soak Christian's hand, he doesn't stop teasing my clit. He keeps pressing down on my ever more sensitive clit, moving me through my climax yet somehow keeping me at the pinnacle of it at the same time.

"Open your eyes. Look at how beautiful you look as you climax," Christian whispers in my ear.

I feel his warm breath tickle my face, and I feel goosebumps chase each other over my skin at his words. I almost dare not look, but I open my eyes and slowly lift my head up. Christian works me eagerly as I watch myself and just when I think my climax is fading, he brings me to the edge once more.

I go hurtling over, watching myself in the mirror as all of my muscles go rigid. My mouth hangs open as I gasp for a breath that doesn't come. I can't bear to watch myself this way and instead, I flick my eyes to Christian. His eyes are on my reflection and I look deep into his eyes in the mirror as I have the most intense orgasm I have ever had.

It's the sort of orgasm I've read about but never quite believed in. The sort that makes my knees buckle and my calf and thigh muscles turn to water. The sort that forces Christian to hold me up although if it worries him, he doesn't show it. It's the sort of orgasm that makes every other orgasm I've ever had seem like comparing a pin prick on the end of a finger to having your arm ripped off.

When Christian finally slips his fingers out from between my lips, I've come almost completely undone. I can't remember the last time I was able to grab a breath. My lungs burn and my vision flickers dangerously. My body aches where every muscle has been held rigid, and my clit throbs from the stimulation, and – dare I admit it – the need for more orgasms like that one.

I'm finally able to breathe again and I suck in a gasping breath that burns my throat and makes my head spin for a moment. Christian has both his arms around my waist and I'm leaning back against him as he nuzzles against my neck. I'm exhausted, physically and mentally, and for a moment as I pant wildly, I let my eyes close.

As I slowly come back to myself, I become aware of Christian's huge hard cock pressing against my ass and suddenly, I don't feel so tired anymore. In fact, I feel ready for anything. I open my eyes and I turn in Christian's arms and kiss him full on the mouth. He moans into my mouth as he kisses me back, enveloping me in his heat. He runs his hands down my back and over the curve of my ass, cupping my ass cheeks in his hands and lifting me. I allow myself to be lifted, wrapping my legs around Christian's waist.

I can feel his cock against my lips now and I am desperate for him to fill me, but it seems he's going to tease me for a little bit longer. He moves his hips so the tip of his cock rubs through my slit, over my clit and back towards my pussy, but just as he is about to slip inside of me, he moves back the other way, rubbing himself across my slick flesh and spreading my juices all around.

He moves then, walking me away from the mirror and taking me to the bed this time. He lays me down on the bed on my back and crawls up quickly, kneeling between my legs for a moment. He looks down at me and he moans, a sound so full of longing I feel my heart skip a beat knowing it is me that made him make that sound.

He moves forward, getting on top of me and I wrap my legs around his waist again. There's no teasing this time. He wastes no time in slamming into me. I gasp as he fills me up and I feel my pussy stretching to accommodate him. I feel a slight sting between my legs as I open further and further for him, but rather than be painful, it feels erotic and it sends me rushing towards my climax once more.

Christian begins to thrust, moving in and out of me and I match his movements thrust for thrust. It feels amazing to be so full and I can feel myself on the edge of another orgasm after a few minutes of us thrusting away together. I try to hold myself back but I can't. My orgasm slams through my body whether I'm ready for it or not.

My pussy clenches, tightening around Christian's cock and making him moan my name in a low, lust filled voice. My clit tingles and my body feels like it's on fire as sparks and explosions erupt through every nerve. I feel a rush of warm wetness as another wave of pleasure coasts over me and again, Christian moans as my slippery flesh grips him and pulls him deeper and deeper inside of me.

As my orgasm fades and Christian's thrusts get harder and faster, an idea comes to me. I'm almost afraid to act on it, scared Christian will think I'm some sort of weirdo, but I tell myself not to be stupid. He'll love it. I want to straddle him, to watch myself do it in the mirror. He encouraged me to watch myself come earlier and I'm sure he would encourage this notion.

Before I can talk myself out of it, I buck my hips and roll to the side, pushing Christian off me. I follow him quickly, rolling him onto his back and straddling him, slipping him back inside of me. I look up and to the side and meet my own eyes in the mirror. A flood of desire rushes over me as I begin to move up and down on Christian's cock, watching myself move.

I look good, even if I do say so myself. My breasts bounce around wildly and Christian reaches up and grabs them, kneading one in each hand, teasing my nipples. I watch his hands in the mirror for a second and then I look back at my face. My gaze flickers between the two scenes as pleasure fills me once more and another orgasm rips through me.

I pant and gasp, moaning Christian's name over and over again as my delicious climax holds me in its grip. I go rigid for a moment, every muscle tightening, and Christian keeps pumping into me, sending me jerking up and down on him, his cock pressing against my g-spot and drawing my climax out.

Christian moves his hands to my hips and he moves me up and down faster and faster until I am a blur in the mirror. As he comes, he holds me in place, pressed down tightly on him so he fills me right up. His face contorts as his own orgasm moves through him and I feel his cock going wild inside of me as he spurts.

Finally, he relaxes his hold on my hips and runs a hand through his hair. He smiles up at me as he pants for breath and I move off him, laying down beside him, also trying to get my breath back.

There is no doubt in my mind that Christian is by far the best lover I have ever had and of course I don't regret having sex with him, but I do kind of regret the way it happened. I was right earlier – I'm really not a one night stand kind of a girl. But that's ok. Maybe Christian wants to see me again. After that mind blowing sex we've just had, surely we'll start dating now.

I'm imagining what it would be like to date someone like Christian as I slowly coast down from my orgasm and recover my senses somewhat. I turn my head to ask Christian what he thinks of the idea, but his eyes are closed and I realize that if he isn't quite asleep yet, he isn't far from it.

I also realize that I've gotten a bit chilly and I shuffle around and pull the duvet out from underneath me and pull it over me. As I snuggle down, Christian rolls over and pulls the duvet onto him too and then he wraps an arm around my waist and gives me a sleepy kiss on the forehead.

His affection puts my mind at rest. Of course we're going to start dating. He just doesn't want to talk about it right now. We'll talk in the morning. I'm still imagining a world where I get to have sex like this every night as I fall asleep in Christian's arms with a smile on my face.

AVA

I wake up and for a moment, I have no idea where I am. The room doesn't look familiar to me at all and then I feel a warm hand on my hip. I stiffen slightly as shock engulfs me. What the fuck? Where am I? And more importantly who is in this bed with me?

In a rush, last night all comes flooding back to me and I relax a little bit. I'm with Christian, the hot guy from last night. I'm in his bed and the bruised feeling between my legs is from where we fucked. It's his hand on my hip and this must be his bedroom, his bed.

I remember it all now, although I kind of wish I didn't. I was so forward, marching up to Christian and making it clear what I wanted. And then after we had sex, I remember being worried that he would only want a one night stand with me, but then he held me as we fell asleep and I realized he wanted more too. And now he's pulling me closer to him again and I was right. He wouldn't do that if he didn't want to give us a chance. He would just be trying to get me to leave.

I shuffle backwards a bit moving into Christian's warmth, pressing my body up against his. He moves against me, fitting himself around me and then he brushes my shoulder with his lips and moves his hand from my hip across my body and over my stomach.

"Good morning," he whispers as his hand moves lower down my body.

"Good morning," I echo, my voice husky with sleep and lust.

Any further words I might have uttered are forgotten as Christian's fingers push between my lips and press against my already tender clit. I gasp in a breath as a mixture of pain and pleasure pulses through my clit. Part of me wants to pull away from Christian's touch because I'm still so sensitive after last night, and the other part of me wants to grind my hips to make his light touch firmer. The latter part of me wins and I roll my hips, moaning out loud as Christian takes the hint and ups the pressure on my clit.

It doesn't take long for the tender, zingy feeling to go away and to be replaced with an entirely more enjoyable feeling. Pleasure pulses from my clit up through my stomach and my pussy aches to be filled by Christian once more.

I can feel his hard cock pressing up against my ass and I know he's as ready for this as I am. I squirm slightly, shifting position to make it easier for Christian to get inside of me. I feel a warm burst of air on my shoulder as Christian laughs softly behind me.

"All in good time," he whispers.

I moan in frustration but it becomes a moan of pleasure part way through as Christian leans in and kisses my neck as his fingers continue to work my clit. He runs his tongue from my ear to the base of my neck and then across my shoulder blade, leaving behind a warm trail that goes cool and sprouts goosebumps as he leaves it behind. Shivers of pleasure course through my body as Christian's fingers work me faster and faster, making me writhe with pleasure beneath his touch. I'm going crazy with the need for release, and before I know it, I go over the edge, tumbling headlong into a delicious orgasm that seems to engulf my whole body in a wave of warm ecstasy.

I gasp for breath as my body goes rigid. My spine arcs and I feel my upper body pressing back against Christian, my head lolling against his shoulder. He slips his fingers out of my lips and presses his palm against my stomach, pressing my ass back against him, teasing me with the feeling of his hard cock once more pressing against me.

As I come back down from my orgasm, my pussy aches to be filled and I lift my upper leg, inviting Christian in. There's no more teasing this time. He takes the invitation. He runs his finger tips over the inside of my thigh and then he takes the weight of my leg and he fills me, slamming into me and making me cry out as his huge cock pushes inside of me.

We begin to move, our bodies moving as one together, both of us in perfect time with each other as we thrust faster and faster. My pussy feels so full and I love the feeling of Christian inside of me, stretching me out to accommodate him. It feels like he is filling a part of me I didn't really realize was empty until now.

After a moment or two, Christian's thrusts become shorter and faster and his breathing becomes ragged, almost painful sounding and I know he's close to climaxing. I tighten my pussy, clenching the muscles there around him and I smile to myself as he moans my name, a sound filled with lust and pleasure. The sound of my name on his lips sends a shiver of pleasure through me.

I feel Christian's cock twitch inside of me as his orgasm hits him and as he starts to come, he presses his fingers roughly against my clit once more, taking me completely by surprise as he begins to work me. His touch is insistent and it pushes me over the edge almost immediately. I was already on the brink of climaxing myself as I was so turned on by hearing my name on Christian's lips that way, and his touch has just completely finished me off.

I feel all of my muscles clench as pleasure runs through my body, lighting up every nerve ending as it goes. I no longer have the energy to hold my leg up and I let it drop. As it drops, my pussy becomes tighter around Christian and he moans my name again as he spurts into me for a second time.

All too soon, it's over and Christian slips out of me. We lie where we are, both of us panting for breath. Christian brings his hand back to my stomach and I rest my own hand on top of it, drawing invisible shapes on the back of his hand with my fingernails.

Already I feel too empty, as though I can feel my pussy crying out for more and I want Christian again. I don't care that I'm sore, or that we have just finished having sex. All I care about right now is having him inside of me again. I can't imagine a time when I'm not ready to have sex with Christian.

I feel my cheeks reddening as my mind runs away with itself, but I don't let the brief flush of embarrassment I feel at my own desire stop me from acting. Not this time. Something about lying here in Christian's bed, about to start something beautiful with him, makes me feel braver than I have ever felt before, and before I can change my mind, I roll over to face Christian.

He smiles at me lazily and I feel my heart skip a beat as I smile back at him. God he's even more gorgeous than I remembered him to be. I bite my bottom lip and look down for a second and then I look back up and into Christian's eyes. He holds my gaze and again, his very presence makes me feel emboldened.

I release my lip from between my teeth and lean forward, closing the gap between Christian and me. I kiss him gently on the lips, my lips barely fluttering over his. It's just enough to make my skin tingle and I know I am not only teasing Christian here; I'm also teasing myself. I kiss him again, harder this time, my movements more insistent. He moans into my mouth and kisses me back and before I know it, we are locked in a passionate kiss that makes my heart swell and my stomach roll with excitement. Christian's hand comes up and rests on my cheek and then he pushes his fingers into my hair as I hold him tightly against me.

Before I can stop myself, I push Christian onto his back. I roll with him, straddling him, not breaking our kiss. I move my hips, rubbing my wet pussy up and down his cock until it springs back to life beneath me. Christian moans into my mouth as I bring him back to life and I feel my heart swell once more.

I shuffle forward slightly and I finally move my lips away from Christian's. I sit up straight and smile down at him. He returns my smile. I reach behind myself and grab his cock in my fist. I begin to move my fist up and down Christian's length and he smiles up at me and folds his hands beneath his head. He closes his eyes as I keep working him. I get into a rhythm, my wrist moving quickly, my grip firm but not uncomfortably so.

I wait, keeping up my rhythm, bringing Christian closer and closer to the edge, and then I lift my body up and move backwards until I'm above him and I come back down hard, impaling myself on Christian's cock, moving my hand away from his length as he penetrates me. His eyes fly open, his expression a mixture of shock and delight.

I smile at him and he shakes his head but he's smiling too and I think he might be shaking his head in wonder. I hope he is. I begin to move up and down on Christian's cock and he moans my name as I ride him. He reaches up and cups my breasts in his hands. I can feel the hardness of my nipples against his palms and his touch sends little jolts of electricity down through my body where they collide with the pulsing nerves of my pussy.

I up the pace of my movement, feeling the climax sizzling inside of me, ready to burst out and set my body on fire once more. Christian moans as I move and the moan is so full of lust and longing that it sends me over the edge.

I feel my pussy clench around Christian's cock and I feel a rush of warm wetness as I come hard. I pause for a moment, filled all of the way up by Christian, my orgasm pulsing through me. I can't think. I can barely breathe. I feel like I'm floating and yet at the same time, I can feel each of my muscles hard and rigid, my tendons straining.

I can feel my mouth opening and closing as I gasp in tiny gulps of air. Christian has his hands on my hips now and he's moving me up and down, my pussy sliding over him once more. His movement breaks the spell and I can breathe again. I pant and gasp but it doesn't stop me from moving on Christian once more, bringing him closer and closer to the edge.

I feel him come inside of me and I watch as his face contorts with ecstasy. He's still for a moment, frozen in a moment of utter pleasure. And the moment passes and he opens his eyes, his face returning to normal. He smiles at me as he slips out of me. I smile down at him and then I climb off him and lay down on my side facing him.

I smile as he turns his head to look at me. I wait for his kiss, but it doesn't come. He watches me, and I can see him starting to look a bit impatient. He must be waiting for me to be the one to speak. I think for a moment and then my smile widens.

"I'm glad I met you," I say.

I hope it's the right balance between letting him know I like him and not coming on too strong.

"Me too," Christian smiles. "Last night was fun Ava. And this morning."

"Yes, it was," I agree. I think for a moment and then I feel suddenly brave and I blurt out exactly what I am thinking. "I was thinking maybe we could have some more fun tonight? Like maybe we could go out for dinner together or something?"

"I don't think so," Christian says. He looks uncomfortable suddenly. "Look Ava like I said, last night was fun. But that's all it can be. I'm not looking for anything more serious than that right now."

"But... I don't understand," I say, shaking my head. "We were good together and you know it."

"Sure we had good sex, I'm definitely not denying that," Christian says. "But it was only ever going to be a one night stand."

"Wow," I say, shaking my head, shocked to hear that my initial fear had been correct. "You mean you used me?"

"No, that's not what I mean at all. At what point did I say this was anything more than what it is?" Christian demands.

He's right. He didn't say anything of the kind, but his actions sure suggested he was seeing what we had as more than just sex. Either that or I have read the entire situation completely wrong. I'm quickly starting to think it's the latter.

"You... I..." I start. I sigh and shake my head and then I start over again. "I'm just saying I'm not a one night stand sort of a girl."

Christian snorts out a laugh.

"You could have fooled me," he says. "You were all over me before you even knew my name last night."

I feel heat rush to my cheeks, a mixture of embarrassment and anger. I'm not sure who I'm angry at. Myself, because Christian's words have a ring of truth to them, or him for pointing it out? Either way, I can't stay here even a moment longer. The humiliation is just too much.

"You utter asshole," I say, pushing the covers back and getting out of Christian's bed.

I'm conscious of the fact that I'm naked but there's not much I can do about that until I find my dress. I spot it on the ground and storm over to it. I bend down to retrieve it and as I do, I glance back and see Christian watching me. I can't read his expression. I don't know if he's amused by me or turned on by me, but either way, I feel heat in my cheeks again, and despite the fact that I'm furious with Christian, I feel desire flood through my body and I can't help but pull my dress over my head slowly, running the fabric over my curves with a deliberate stroking motion.

Ignoring the tingling in my clit, I glance around until I spot my bra. I grab it from the ground and push my feet into my heels. I keep looking around, but I can't spot my panties anywhere and the longer I stay here, the more embarrassing it's becoming. While I don't particularly like the idea of leaving my dirty panties here in a virtual stranger's house, it seems like a better idea than having to suffer the humiliation of getting down on my hands and knees to look beneath the bed, because that's surely the only place they could have gotten to.

The decision made, I grab my purse from the ground and head for the door. I don't look back at Christian. I can't bear to see the look on his face. I don't need to look anyway; I can imagine the contempt there, or worse, the amusement. In the cold light of day, Christian seems like a very different person to the one who snuggled up against me last night. I mean sure, I can accept that I got the wrong end of the stick and thought there was more to this than there is. But that doesn't give Christian the right to laugh at me. And it certainly doesn't give him the right to imply that I throw myself at anyone and everyone.

I'd like to think he was joking, just trying to lighten the mood and picked a bad way to do it, but I don't think that's the case at all. If it was, surely he would have said something by now. An apology maybe, or maybe him saying I don't have to go. But he hasn't so much as uttered a word, and he doesn't - not even when I storm across the room and leave it, slamming the bedroom door behind me hard enough to make it shake in its frame.

I retrace the steps I took last night – along the hallway and down the stairs – but I have a very different feeling inside of myself now. Last night I felt giddy on life, excited and turned on and ready for anything. Now I just feel deflated. I can feel tears prickling behind my eyes and it's all I can do not to let them fall. I won't let myself cry over Christian.

I reach the front door. I pause for a moment to stuff my bra into my purse – the walk of shame I'm about to do is going to be embarrassing enough without me doing it with a bra in my hand. I tell myself that's the only reason I'm pausing here in Christian's hallway, that it's not because I'm not secretly hoping to hear him calling my name and coming after me.

Even if that is what I'm doing, and it definitely isn't, it doesn't matter, because Christian isn't coming. He isn't shouting my name. He isn't saying he's sorry. And he's most definitely not begging me for a chance to make this right.

I pull the front door open and step outside. Fuck him. He had his chance. I'm not going to waste any more time thinking about him. Not even a little bit. I pull the door closed behind me and look around. I didn't remember this estate wrong from last night. The houses here are huge and this is one upmarket estate.

I know I need to call a cab as I have no real idea how to get back to the part of the city where normal people live, and I have a decision to make. Do I call from right here on Christian's doorstep and risk the humiliation of having him see me here? Or do I leave his property and call for a cab when I'm out of sight and risk one of Christian's neighbors calling the cops because I clearly don't belong here?

I choose the latter. I'd rather have an embarrassing encounter with a cop than have another one with Christian. I start down the garden path and slip through it. I head towards what I think might be the main road if my memory of last night's journey is correct.

I can still feel the tears in my eyes threatening to fall and I remind myself that I'm not meant to be thinking about Christian any more. This thought does nothing to move the lump that's blocking my throat, yet as I tell myself that Christian isn't worth my tears, I realize something. The urge to cry isn't really about him. It's about me. Yes, Christian and I had amazing sex. Yes, he's hot as hell. But he showed his true colours this morning after he had gotten what he wanted and I have no intention of chasing after some asshole guy who thinks it's ok to treat people that way.

No, this thick feeling in my throat is all about me. The urge to cry is because I feel like I've let myself down. I can tell myself all I want to that I thought there was something special between Christian and me, but the fact is, I went up to a stranger in a night club and made it clear I was available for the night. Christian didn't really take advantage of me. No, it was more like he took what I was offering him.

And that's what upsets me. I've always been the kind of person who wants some sort of connection and commitment with a guy before I jump into bed with him. I wasn't kidding when I told Christian I'm not a one night stand kind of a girl. And yet here I am, on a walk of shame to somewhere I recognize enough to be able to call a cab and tell the dispatcher what street I'm on.

I sigh and shake my head. I don't know what's wrong with me. Plenty of girls my age sleep around and they don't seem to feel any regrets about it. It's not like we're living in the 1950's for goodness sake. There is nothing wrong with enjoying sex and choosing to have sex with a guy just because I want to.

I start to feel better as I tell myself that. It's not like I'm going to make a habit of picking up strangers at clubs and going home with them, but maybe this is a rite of passage to some extent. Like it's something that I had to experience, even if it is just the once. I mean I am twenty four. Maybe it's past time I let my hair down and live a little bit.

I can feel myself starting to smile a little. When I let go of the self-inflicted shame, I realize there's actually nothing to be ashamed about. We were two consenting adults who had a bit of fun together. It's actually quite liberating to just admit that. And yes, it helps me to feel better because it suddenly occurred to me that I never have to see Christian again and no one else needs to know what happened last night.

CHRISTIAN

I wash away the soap from my body and along with it, I rinse away the sweet scent of Ava's body. I kind of wish I could wash away the guilty feeling inside of myself along with the soap suds. I didn't mean to upset her this morning. What I said was just an automatic response to what I thought was her making a joke, and trying to lighten the mood. I thought she would laugh along with me, maybe pretend to be offended and playfully slap me. I didn't expect her to actually be offended.

I probably should have apologized for what I said, but honestly, when Ava leapt up from my bed, I was taken by surprise. And then as she bent down to retrieve her dress from the floor, the view was far too good to ignore. By the time she was covered again and had her bra in her hand and her shoes on, she hadn't so much as looked at me and I felt as though the moment to apologize had passed. At that point, it would have felt fake, and besides, she had made it pretty clear she didn't want to talk to me and I wasn't about to beg her to accept my apology.

Plus, if I'm being completely honest, I couldn't help but ask myself what the point of apologizing to her was anyway. It would only give Ava false hope that we could be something more than what we had been, and we can't. I don't have time for a relationship and even if I did, I couldn't imagine being with someone like Ava. She's kind of uptight if her inability to laugh at herself is anything to go on and that's the last thing I need.

I kind of got the impression she'd be a little bit clingy too. The way she wanted us to go for dinner tonight – even if I wanted more that would have been way too soon. No, I have definitely dodged a bullet there and luckily, I won't ever have to see Ava again.

The fact that I let her leave without even attempting to go after her and apologize to her tells me that she's not going to try and look me up. And I'm certainly not going to be looking her up. So that's that then. I've had a lucky escape and I'm pleased that Ava is out of my life.

And if I tell myself that enough times, then maybe Ava will get out of my goddamned head as well as out of my life.

AVA

Three Months Later

I smile to myself as I end the call and start to type the new appointment into Mr. Kramer's online diary. He's been wanting to set up a meeting with Joe Lancaster since the rumors started that he is unhappy with his current representation, and he's not the only one. Pretty much every lawyer in the city has been trying and failing to get a meeting with Joe Lancaster. And I haven't failed. I got the appointment for Mr. Kramer. He's going to be so happy.

I finish adding the details to Mr. Kramer's schedule and then I stand up and move out from behind my desk and approach Mr. Kramer's office. His office is right beside my desk, a strategic move so I can screen who does and doesn't get an audience with Mr. Kramer. I send away most of the people who stop by because I know Mr. Kramer is a very busy man who doesn't like to be disturbed unless it's a planned appointment or something urgent has come up. Normally, I wouldn't be about to go and disturb him myself for any other reason, but I know he will want to know about this right now.

I know he won't refuse an audience with me because he knows I would never disturb him if it wasn't urgent. Or in this case, damned good news that needs to be shared immediately. I tap on his door and wait for him to shout for me to come in. My body is zinging with nervous excitement.

"Come in," I hear Mr. Kramer call from inside of his office.

I smile and then I push the door open and slip inside, closing it quietly behind me. I can't stop myself from grinning and I'm sure I look like I've lost it a little bit.

Mr. Kramer is sitting behind his large oak desk. He's typing something and he finishes with a flourish and then he looks up and smiles quizzically at me, most likely because he's wondering why I'm standing here with this goofy grin on my face.

Mr. Kramer is in his fifties, around fifty-five I would say, but he's aged well. In his expensive, tailored suit, and with the youthful twinkle in his eye, he could easily pass for a decade younger than he is. The only tiny clue to his being older than a person would assume at first glance is the slight greying of his hair around his temples.

"What can I do for you Ava?" Mr. Kramer asks.

"We did it," I squeak. "You've got a meeting tomorrow afternoon with Joe Lancaster."

"Holy shit," Mr. Kramer says. His smile becomes a soft laugh and he shakes his head. "I always knew you were the best secretary here Ava, but this proves it beyond any reasonable doubt."

I feel myself flushing slightly underneath his praise. I know I'm good at my job, but hearing Mr. Kramer confirm that is always good.

"Thank you, Mr. Kramer," I say.

Mr. Kramer has been telling me to call him Jeff ever since I became his personal secretary but it just doesn't feel right and he's now pretty much given up on getting me to do it. He still rolls his eyes when I say Mr. Kramer though.

"I'm certain now that I'm making the right decision," he adds, his expression turning thoughtful.

"The right decision about what?" I ask. He nods to the chair opposite him and I sit down. "I was going to call you in here soon to talk to you anyway so we might as well make it now."

I instantly feel a pit of dread in my stomach, although I have no idea why. I have done nothing to warrant being told off and after the score with Joe Lancaster, if I had made a mistake, I think it would have been all forgiven and forgotten. Mr. Kramer must be able to read the worry on my face, because he smiles reassuringly at me.

"Don't look so worried Ava," he says. "You're not in any trouble or anything."

I relax slightly, and give Mr. Kramer an embarrassed smile. I've got to find a way to stop showing my every thought on my face.

"I've been considering this for a while now, and I think the time is right for me to leave the company," Mr. Kramer says.

I feel my jaw drop. I did not see this coming. Not even a little bit. Mr. Kramer lives for his job.

"I… I don't understand. Why would you leave?" I blurt out.

I know I'm probably crossing a line asking such a personal question of him, but it's out before I consider it. Besides, he wouldn't be discussing this with me if he didn't want me to know about it, and he must have known that I would ask why he's leaving.

"I've dedicated most of my working life to this company, and as my wife continues to point out, that's been pretty much a waste of time if I don't sit back and enjoy the rewards of my hard work at some point," Mr. Kramer says.

My head is spinning with all of this. I can fully understand why Mr. Kramer and his wife have come to the decision they have, but I'm nervous once again. Perhaps it's a little bit selfish of me to not be happier for Mr. Kramer, but right now, I'm just worried about the uncertainty of my own position and questions rattle through my head one after the other on a loop.

What will happen to me now? Will I be fired? Moved back to the general secretary's pool? Mr. Foley, the other partner, has his own secretary and I assume whoever Mr. Kramer is promoting will bring his or her own secretary with them. Will I just be tossed aside like trash and left to find something else? And if that happens, will I be expected to pay back the money for my degree? It was a caveat that if I left within five years of qualifying, I would have to pay back the money, or if I got fired. But surely this is different. It's not like I'm going to get fired for anything I've done wrong.

Some of the nerves are starting to turn to anger. Am I really going to end up in almost fifty thousand dollars worth of debt because Mr. Kramer leaves the company?

"You look more than a little bit pissed off Ava," Mr. Kramer says. "What is it? What's wrong?"

"I'm sorry," I say automatically. But then I think about it and I shake my head. "No actually, I'm not sorry. I have a right to be a bit annoyed if I'm about to lose my job through no fault of my own and then have to pay back a ton of money for a degree that you pushed me to go for."

"Wow. I must admit I'm a little bit upset that you seem to think so little of me Ava," Mr. Kramer says.

"Sorry," I say again, and this time, I do mean it. I actually think very highly of Mr. Kramer. I look down at my lap and then I look up again. "So I don't have to pay back the money?"

"No, of course not. And you're not losing your job either," Mr. Kramer says. "Keeping you in your current position is non-negotiable even after I am gone."

"But won't the partner you promote want to bring their own secretary to the role?" I ask.

I don't want to be left in a position where the new managing partner doesn't want me working at his or her desk and his or her old secretary hates me for taking the job they thought would be theirs.

"I'm not promoting someone in house," Mr. Kramer says, surprising me once more. "It's always been a known thing with Matthew Foley and me that when I move on, my son will be taking over my position. My son is a well respected lawyer and the only reason he has never worked at this firm before is because he wanted to get out there and experience working somewhere where he wasn't just seen as the boss's son. He wanted to prove to me and I think himself that he had what it takes to make it without any favors."

I nod my head. I can fully understand why he would want to do that. If my father ran a law firm, I would probably feel the same way and not want to work for him either.

"And your son is ok with keeping me on as his personal secretary?" I ask.

"Of course. As I said it's non-negotiable, but you're one of the best legal secretaries we have, Ava and my son should just be happy to be working alongside you," Mr Kramer says.

I start to relax a little bit. As much as I enjoy working for Mr. Kramer and I will be sad to see him go, I will still have my job and for that I am grateful. There won't be any need for me to move departments and no one is going to be glaring daggers at me thinking I've taken their job. And surely if Mr. Kramer trusts his son to take over running his half of the company, he can't be awful or anything.

"Thank you," I say.

Mr. Kramer nods his head and then he looks thoughtful for a moment.

"I suppose if we sign Joe he's going to be Chris's client rather than mine now. I think I might take him along to the meeting tomorrow and then we'll come back here afterwards and you can meet him," Mr. Kramer says. "Meet Chris, my son, I mean, not Joe."

I smile and nod my head. I would definitely prefer to meet Mr. Kramer's son and get a bit of a feel for him before we start working together. I guess tomorrow is going to be pretty interesting.

~

I look up and smile as I spot Mr. Kramer walking towards his office from the elevator. I feel a flutter of nerves in my stomach. This is it. The moment I'm going to meet his son and know whether working for him is going to be a chore or not. God I hope we get along, I think to myself, and not for the first time. My mind goes blank as I search for Mr. Kramer's son's name. It will be so embarrassing if I'm expected to know it and I don't. I know Mr. Kramer said it yesterday when we discussed this meeting. What is it? What is it?

It comes to me in a sudden rush of inspiration. Christopher! Oh thank God. Yes, it's Christopher.

As I slowly recover from my panic over the almost forgotten name of my new boss, I realize that Mr. Kramer is alone. I don't know whether to feel relieved or disappointed that I'm obviously not going to get to meet Christopher right now.

Mr. Kramer stops at my desk and grins at me and I know he's only gone and done it. For him to look this happy, he's signed Joe Lancaster. He has to have, or he would have come in with a face like thunder. For the moment, meeting my new boss is the last thing on my mind.

"You did it?" I say, already sure he has but needing to be certain.

"We sure did Ava. Joe Lancaster is officially the newest client of Kramer and Foley," Mr. Kramer grins. He raises his palm and I high five him.

"Nice one," I say. "I knew you could get him on board."

Mr. Kramer smiles.

"It's been a long time coming but I got there in the end," he says. He pauses and then he nods towards his office door. "Come into my office."

I stand up and follow Mr. Kramer to his office. He glances back at me as we enter.

"Chris is just getting parked and then he'll be up," he says. "The parking lot is pretty full so it could take a while."

Mr. Kramer gestures towards the armchairs sitting around a glass coffee table in the corner of his office. I smile and go and take a seat, choosing one facing the door so I can get a glimpse of his son as soon as he enters the room and hopefully get a feel for him. Mr. Kramer goes over to his desk and starts rummaging around in his drawers muttering to himself as he searches for something.

The office door opens before Mr. Kramer finds whatever it is that he's looking for in his desk drawers and I watch as what has to be his son enters the office. I know it has to be his son because no one else would dare to march into Mr. Kramer's office without knocking, even if I'm not at my desk.

I glance at Christopher as he closes the office door behind him, hoping to quickly size him up before he catches me looking at him. My heart sinks and I feel heat rush to my face when I see who it is. The moment seems to go into slow motion. This can't be happening to me. It has to be some sort of a nightmare. Yes, that's it. It's a nightmare and I'm about to wake up. Except it's not a nightmare. It's very real and I don't know how it happened.

Except I do. Now that I think about it, Mr. Kramer only ever referred to his son as Chris. I assumed that it came from Christopher, but I was wrong. Because Christopher isn't the only name that can be shortened to Chris. No, Christian can also be shortened to Chris. And the man who has stepped into the office is definitely named Christian, and somewhere, back at his house, is a pair of my used panties unless he's already found them and thrown them away.

My cheeks are burning hot and I just know they would be glaringly red if it wasn't for the foundation I'm wearing. As it stands, even with the makeup I know I'll look pink, but hopefully I can play that off as excitement about the Lancaster contract.

Christian closes the office door behind him, breaking the slow motion spell and allowing things to move normally once more. He doesn't slam the door closed but he closes it firmly and it makes enough of a noise that Mr. Kramer pops up from behind his desk. He smiles at Christian and stands up properly and moves around the desk. I remind myself that my expression usually gives away exactly what I'm feeling and I make a point of keeping my face neutral. God this is hard.

"Ava, this is my son and the new managing partner here, Christian Kramer," Mr. Kramer says. "Christian, this is Ava Long. She's my personal secretary and once you take over the firm, she'll be yours."

I know Mr. Kramer only means I'll be Christian's secretary but still, the way he says I'll be his sends a shiver through me. I ignore it and force myself to smile at Christian. He returns my smile with a beaming smile of his own, and if he's in the least bit perturbed by all of this, he's hiding it much better than I am.

"Pleased to meet you," he says, covering the gap between us and extending his hand to me. I jump to my feet and shake his hand, trying not to think of what those hands are capable of. "Sorry, Ava was it?"

I nod my head mutely. Was that all part of the act for his father's benefit or does he genuinely not remember me? As painful as it is to even think it, I think it has to be the latter. Mr. Kramer obviously has no idea that Christian and I slept together like three months ago and he has no reason to suspect anything just because Christian remembers my name the first time he is told it. I feel myself blushing again and I feel a tightening in my throat. For a horrible minute I feel like I'm going to cry or retch or something equally embarrassing, but I swallow hard, swallowing away the ball of sorrow in my throat.

So Christian doesn't remember me. So what? It's not like I want to ever sleep with him again. And it might actually be less awkward if he doesn't remember me. And I will try to make my peace with the fact that it probably means that Christian has one night stands like that regularly and I really was nothing more than another fuck to him. Ugh. I hate him.

"Christian will be shadowing me for the rest of this week," Mr. Kramer says to me, forcing me out of the little pity party I'm throwing for myself in my head and back into the room. "And then from next week, he'll be taking over completely.

He will need your help to settle in and learn the routine we follow here. Am I correct in assuming I can trust you to have his back Ava?"

"Yes," I say nodding my head. "Of course."

In this moment, I honestly don't know if I'm making a promise I can keep or not, but I do know that Mr. Kramer has always had my back and I owe him enough that I will at least try to work alongside Christian without any friction. I really don't want to let Mr. Kramer down, not after everything he has done for me. I will just have to live with this being slightly awkward until it isn't anymore.

I decide that it seemingly not being awkward for Christian is actually making it more awkward for me. If we were both awkward, then we could talk about it quickly and leave it in the past. If it's only me who is awkward, it makes me look like an immature kid who doesn't know how to handle sex while Christian comes across as the grown up. And I couldn't stand the humiliation if I bring it up and he outright admits that he doesn't recognize me.

God I need to get out of this office. It suddenly feels too small, too hot and too crowded. I tell myself not to be silly. If I can't get through this, then what chance have I got of getting through work every day? I sit back down rather heavily and force myself to return Christian's smile, a smile I earn by agreeing to have his back.

We talk for a few more minutes about how things are going to work, but really, there isn't a lot to talk about. The setup here is pretty much standard to any law firm and Christian seems like he has enough experience to be able to mostly hit the ground running. I'm relieved when Mr. Kramer smiles at me and tells me I can leave now, that he and Christian have a few personal matters to discuss. I stand up and Christian stands up with me. He extends his hand once more, his friendly smile back in place.

"Thank you," he says as I shake his outstretched hand. "It's been a pleasure meeting you and I'm sure we'll work well together."

I nod mutely. I'm not so sure that's true, but I'm hardly going to say that in front of Mr. Kramer. I scurry away the second Christian releases my hand and I leave the office. I close the door behind me and lean back against it for a moment, taking a deep breath. I push away from the door and go back to my desk.

Fucking hell that was intense. I made my peace with having a one night stand by telling myself I would never have to encounter Christian again. Yet here he is, large as life and being encountered by me. Fuck. I wish I could handle it casually like he is. Nonchalance is an understatement for the way he's behaving. But I'm the opposite. I feel like I need to explain to him all over again that I am not the sort of girl that does stuff like that usually. Any liberation I found in the moment is gone now and I'm back to regretting the sex entirely.

Well, not entirely exactly. I mean the sex was amazing. Easily the best sex I've ever had. But it can never happen again. I can never forget the way Christian laughed at the thought of me not being a one night stand sort of a girl, and I don't think I'll ever quite forgive him for not at least trying to apologize after he said that.

He is arrogant, cold, smug and everything I hate in a man. But then again, he was all of those things three months ago and yet I still ended up in his bed then. And while I won't let that happen again, surely it won't hurt to let myself imagine how amazing it would feel, right?

CHRISTIAN

As the office door closes behind Ava, I feel myself relax, the tension leaving my shoulders and back. I know I played my part well enough that my dad will never think there was anything strange there, but I will still feel better once she's gone. I don't want to mess this job up and the last thing I need is Ava hanging around me, a constant reminder of the fact that I was hardly nice to her after we hooked up.

"She seems nice. It's a shame she'll have to go," I say.

"Go? Go where?" my dad says with a frown.

Ok, I was right to test the water. He likes Ava. I can't suggest firing her then. Not yet at least.

"I don't know," I say feigning innocence. "To whichever partner could use the extra pair of hands I guess."

My dad keeps frowning at me and I realize he's waiting for me to elaborate.

"I'll be hiring my own secretary and I hardly need two," I say. "I don't want to come in looking like the big I am with two secretaries."

My dad is shaking his head before I even reach the end of that sentence.

"The company has just paid for Ava to complete a degree as a legal assistant. I'm not wasting that kind of money by sending her somewhere else. And besides, she's damned good at her job. You won't find a better hire than the one you already have," he says. I start to open my mouth but he doesn't give me a chance to interrupt him. "This isn't open to discussion Chris. It's written into the contract you'll be signing. Ava will be your secretary, end of story. And she's been with me for a long time. I know her well enough to know she isn't the quitting type so let's not get any bright ideas about making her life miserable enough that she quits. In fact, if Ava quits within the first year of you taking over here, then you're out."

"What?" I say. "That's ridiculous."

My dad raises an eyebrow and I sigh. I can see he's serious about this and I have no choice but to accept Ava as my secretary. I'll just have to hope the awkwardness between us shifts quickly. But I'm not about to agree to being beholden to whether or not Ava wants to work here. I'm not petty enough to try to push her out, but what if she decides she doesn't want to have to see me every day and leaves?

"Look, she can stay and be my secretary," I say. "But I can't control whether or not she chooses to leave. What if she meets Mr. Right and he's from Europe and she wants to go live there? Or what if she suddenly decides she wants a different career?"

"You know what I'm saying Chris," my dad says. "Just make damned sure she's happy here."

I nod my head. For my dad to be this insistent on her staying, she must be damned good. Surely if I keep up the act of not remembering her, she'll get past the awkwardness quickly enough. As if I could forget her though. I mean yes, she was clingy and uptight and she kind of ruined everything the way she left things, but my God that woman made my body sing in a way no one ever has before. And she made me crave her touch, the thoughts of her staying in my mind long after she was gone from my home.

"Right. Now that the easy bit is out of the way, let's move on to the other condition," my dad says.

"Other condition?" I say.

It's my turn to raise an eyebrow. What's next? Is he going to demand I take on his gardener or something?

"You're thirty now and your mom and I feel like it's time you started growing up and settling down," my dad says.

I can't help but laugh and my dad frowns.

"Are you being serious right now? I have my own house, already bought and paid for, I have plenty of money saved up and I have a good pension and good insurance. How much more grown up do you want me to be?" I say.

I'm actually quite surprised he doesn't think I'm grown up. Most guys my age don't have their shit anywhere near as together as I have mine.

"Don't worry son, I know when it comes to money, you have your head screwed on really tight, there's no denying that. And I'm well aware of your professional achievements. But there's one area of your life where you need to get moving and that's your personal life," my dad says. "We feel like it's time for you to stop playing the field and find a nice woman and settle down."

"This is a joke right?" I say. One look at my dad's face tells me it's not a joke though. I shake my head. "Look with all due respect, it's called my personal life for a reason. It's personal. I don't want to find a woman and settle down and do the whole two point four children and a dog thing. I'm happy the way I am. I don't have time for a relationship."

"Then make time," my dad says. "I don't want you to wake up one day and realize that somewhere along the way, you got old and you're still alone and regret that you never found anyone to share your life with."

"That's not going to happen," I say.

"I know," my dad says with a smile that I don't like one little bit. "Because I'm going to make sure it doesn't. Which brings me onto the other condition of you taking over my half of this company. You will have one year to find the right girl and settle down with her. If, at the end of one year, you haven't done that, then control of the company will all go to Matthew Foley's son."

Fuck. My dad knows exactly which buttons to press when it comes to getting me to do things his way. I was just about ready to tell him to keep his job and go back to working at my old firm. I was a senior partner there and I know they would have me back in a heartbeat, and in five or ten years, I could easily become a named partner there. But now he's made it personal. Because if there's one guy I really fucking hate it's Lewis Foley, Matthew Foley's son.

The guy is everything that's wrong with the world. He's self-centered, entitled, a brat really. He's also arrogant and he thinks he's better than everyone else. And there is no way in hell I'm about to sit back and let him take over this company. It's bad enough that at some point he will get his own father's half of it. There's no way in hell he's getting my father's half of it.

"Well played Dad," I say, unable to stop myself from grinning slightly in admiration.

My dad laughs and nods his head.

"I figured that would do it," he says. "But listen Chris. Please don't think this is some sort of punishment. And definitely don't think of it as some sort of game. I have put the stakes in there only because I know you would never have agreed to it otherwise, but your mom and I really do want to see you settled down and happy."

I feel my good humor at my dad's getting one over on me fade away slightly as anger over takes me once more.

"What you mean is you want to see me settled down so you two can be happy. I'm already happy and I don't see how complicating things by settling down is going to do anything except make me miserable," I say.

My words don't have the effect I was expecting. My dad laughs softly.

"That's because you haven't ever let yourself get close enough to someone to see how happy it can make you. When you find the one, and you let her into your heart, you'll know what I mean and you'll thank me for it. Just like I thanked your grandfather," he says.

My shock must show on my face because my dad laughs again and nods his head.

"Yup," he says. "I was given pretty much the same deal from my father when I took over from him. And at the time, I thought like you did – love would just complicate things and I was happy without it as long as I had my work. It was only once I met your mother that I realized what true happiness is. And that's all I want for you."

I sigh. This truly is the last thing I want. But I won't let Lewis Foley take what is rightfully mine. And truth be told, I don't want to let my dad down either. I kind of wish I hadn't acted like I didn't know Ava now though, because it's not going to be easy finding a girlfriend when the girl I slept with and then pissed off three months ago is the one running my calendar. I would have liked to have been able to explain that little obstacle, but it's too late now. I made my choice and now I'll just have to live with it.

CHRISTIAN

I t's been just over a week since my dad officially left the firm and I found myself in his old position – in charge of half of the firm. It's been a big adjustment for me – not only do I still have my own clients to represent, I also now have responsibility for the clients of the partners too and if they need help, I'm now their go to guy – but I knew what I was getting into with the work side of things when I agreed to take the position. It was the rest of my dad's deal that had surprised me.

I refuse to think about that right now. I just want to focus on the job. So far, I have enjoyed doing it despite how much more work it is than my previous job. I love a challenge and I feel like I'm rising to this one. The partners all seem decent enough both at their jobs and as people, and if there's any animosity about me getting this job, they are hiding it well.

The phone on my desk rings. I look at the screen and see it's an internal call. It's most likely Ava. I pick up the phone.

"Yeah," I say.

"Just a reminder that you have a meeting in half an hour with Amber Clyde from Clyde's Hospitality," Ava says to me. I open my mouth to ask her for the details, but she beats me to it. "Amber is the owner of the company, an agency that provides staff for hospitality venues. She is currently being sued because one of her people allegedly stole from one of the venues."

"Allegedly?" I say.

"Yes. It hasn't actually been proven yet, although he has been arrested and it looks likely he will plead guilty. We need to prove that Amber did her due diligence and that there was nothing in his history to suggest he would do this," Ava says.

"Got it," I say. "Have Carl sit in on the meeting with us please."

I hang up the telephone and think for a moment. Yeah, it makes sense to have Carl in the meeting. Amber is a big client and she needs to see that we're taking this seriously, hence the reason I'm taking the meeting with her personally, but if the truth be told, going over the guy's background and checking Amber did the same is something my associate can do. Hell it's something Ava could do. It really wouldn't be the best use of my time, showing Amber my face in the meeting will be more than enough to reassure her.

Thinking of Ava brings a smile to my face and I shake my head, quickly stopping myself from smiling. What the fuck was that all about? I suppose it's only fair really though. I'm not above admitting my mistakes and it was a mistake to think that Ava would be anything but professional.

She's a damned good legal secretary and my dad was right to not want to let her go. She's adjusted to working for me instead of my dad with seeming ease and not only has she not dropped the ball, she hasn't let me drop it either and I don't suppose that's been an easy task for her. She's made my settling into this role a whole lot easier, of that I have no doubt.

The awkwardness I expected to feel between us seems to have faded if it was ever there at all. I still haven't come clean about recognizing Ava – I think at this point it will just be awkward and she seems happy to play along too. It's probably for the best that we both pretend not to remember each other, because if we admit it, then who knows what might happen.

Even now with a layer of pretence between us, it's hard to look at Ava and not remember how she felt in my arms or how her pussy felt wrapped tightly around my cock. I shake my head again, shaking away the images as I feel a wave of desire come over me. I can't let myself go there, not even for a second.

I try to remember the way Ava reacted before she left my apartment instead of remembering the fun part. That pretty much does it. It reminds me of how clingy she was and how immature she turned out to be. Not like my date tonight.

At thirty six, Natalie is six years older than me. She's pretty – I mean she's not drop dead gorgeous like Ava – but she's far from ugly. She's attractive, always dressed impeccably and she has a body most men would kill to spend a night with. I guess though that those men probably haven't seen Ava's body – they don't know what they're missing out on.

Natalie, a lawyer I met while working for my old firm, is smart and funny and I always had a soft spot for her, but I always avoided showing it because we worked together. And now that I finally have a date with her, I should be happy, but I'm not really and I can't put my finger on why.

One thing I do know – it's certainly not because every time my mind wanders and I find myself comparing Natalie to Ava, Natalie comes up short every damned time.

M y cell phone rings on the desk beside me. I glance at the screen and see its Sophie calling me. I debate what to do; whether or not I should take the call. Technically I'm at work, so I probably shouldn't be taking a personal call, but at the same time, it's five thirty and while I won't complain about still being here – working late is a part of this job and I knew that going into it – I am officially off the clock. I know Mr. Kramer wouldn't have objected to me taking the call at this time, but I don't really know how Christian will feel about it.

Oh fuck it, I think to myself. If Christian sees me on this call and he has a problem with it, I'm sure he'll make it known and then at least I'll know for next time and I won't do it again. I reach for my cell phone and swipe up to take the call before I can change my mind.

"Hello," I say.

"Ava, hi," Sophie says.

She sounds breathless, like she's been running. She's excited about something. She always sounds breathless when she's excited. I grin to myself. She had a big job interview last week. She must have gotten the job.

"Did you get it?" I say.

"Get what?" Sophie asks.

I can picture her frown of confusion from the questioning tone in her voice.

"The job you applied for," I say, feeling a little bit confused myself now. How can she not know what I mean when that's what she's called me about?

"Oh. That. No, I didn't get it. But nevermind about that. I got something way better," Sophie says.

Ok, that explains her confusion. My own confusion melts away into curiosity. What has she got that's way better than the job she so badly wanted this time last week and now doesn't seem to care about one way or the other?

"Come on then, spill it. The suspense is killing me," I laugh.

Sophie's excitement is contagious. What can she have found that is so amazing she doesn't seem to care she didn't land her dream job? Maybe she's got an offer with a higher salary. Or maybe she's got an offer somewhere exotic like Paris or Rome.

"I've got a date for this weekend," Sophie says. She pauses and I wait for the rest. I realize, a beat too late, that there isn't any more. She sounds deflated, her excitement mostly gone when she speaks again. "You don't exactly sound like you're happy for me."

"What? No. I mean I am happy for you," I say quickly. "I'm just a little bit surprised, that's all. I mean you've had plenty of dates and you've never called me this excited about one before."

"This is different," Sophie says, her voice sounding far away and dreamy, the sort of thing I always thought was fake in movies but apparently isn't. "I think he might be the one you know. He's gorgeous Ava. He looks like a surfer type, all blonde hair and a proper tan."

That's not my type but it certainly sounds like Sophie's type. I can't help but get caught up in her enthusiasm once more and I giggle along with her as she debates what to wear. We chat for a while, going back and forth on Sophie's outfit choices and then her telling me all about the new trendy restaurant he's taking her to. She genuinely does sound happy and I really think she's not that worried about not getting the job she wanted. At least I hope she's really happy and this isn't some sort of really early mid-life crisis.

I decide it's not a crisis, she's just genuinely happy and so when I have to end the call, I don't feel quite so guilty. I wait until five forty five, the very latest I can leave it, and then I tell her I have to go because I need to remind Christian about his meeting in five minutes.

"So he's this big shot lawyer, meant to be all clever and everything and he can't even remember a simple meeting by himself?" Sophie says.

"He has more important things to think about," I say. "That's why it's my job to take care of stuff like that."

"To take care of him you mean. Watch yourself Ava. He'll have you ironing his shirts and cooking his dinner next," Sophie says.

I laugh even though I am a little bit hurt, but it sounds fake and I drop the pretence.

"I did the same job for Mr. Kramer and you didn't give me shit then," I point out.

"True," Sophie agrees. "But when you used to talk about Mr. Kramer, you didn't get that sing-song tone in your voice that you get when you talk about Christian."

She says Christian in a long, drawn out voice, her tone lilting. I feel myself blush slightly and I'm glad she can't see me.

"You're being ridiculous. I don't even like the man," I point out.

"Whatever," Sophie says. "Anyway, you had better go. You don't want to be a naughty girl and need your boss to punish you, do you?"

"Jeez Sophie," I hiss, feeling my face burning with embarrassment, but I'm too late. She's already ended the call.

I put my cell phone back away and take a calming breath. I pick up the desk phone and call through to Christian's office. I remind him about the partner meeting at six and then I hang up.

Is Sophie right? Not about me being into Christian. I mean he's still hot, but I know now what a dick he is when it comes to women, so I would never go there again. But is she right about him being too reliant on me? Am I going above and beyond for Christian?

I don't think I am. I don't think I've done anything for Christian that I didn't do for Mr. Kramer. In fact, I think if anything, I do slightly less for Christian because he tends to take a lot of the calls Mr. Kramer would have wanted fielding.

I think I'm just being paranoid because of Sophie's teasing, because the truth is, this has been going well, much better than I expected it to. Christian seems to have settled in quickly and his routine isn't so dissimilar to his father's that I haven't been able to adapt to it quickly and easily. And while Christian might be a disrespectful ass to women outside of work, here in the office, he has shown me respect and not been an asshole. I guess I can't really ask for much more than that.

Well there is one thing I could ask for, and that's to not have to plan Christian's love life for him. One of my tasks for today was to make a restaurant reservation for Christian for two people at eight o'clock. The restaurant isn't the sort of place someone would take a client – it's definitely a more intimate, date type of restaurant – and Christian told me to use his personal credit card details with the booking rather than his expenses account one.

I suppose I could refuse to do it, but that will only make me look ridiculous, like I'm somehow jealous that Christian has dates because I know after speaking to some of the other secretaries that it's pretty standard practice to organize stuff like this, I just hadn't realized because Mr. Kramer was married. I always thought I was doing him a personal favor when I ordered flowers for his wife's birthday or for Valentine's day but I guess I wasn't. At least I don't have to buy gifts for whoever Christian is dating. Yet. Ugh, enough of that.

Besides I think, smiling to myself at the thought of ordering flowers on Christian's behalf, even if I was jealous, I would have no need to be. As if Mr. I Don't Want a Serious Relationship is going to see this poor girl more than once. I'll just have to try not to remember how our night ended – how he made my body feel things I didn't even know it was possible to feel - because I might not be jealous but I still don't want to think of Christian with some other girl the way he was with me.

Christian's office door opens and I force myself to focus on being professional. I flash him a smile, hoping he can't read my thoughts on my face.

"Your reservation for tonight has been confirmed," I tell him.

"Good. Thank you," he says. "See you tomorrow Ava."

I smile and nod my head and then I watch as he walks off towards the conference room and I can't help but admire his ass as he goes. I try to go back to what I was doing, but my mind is suddenly full of Christian, and the more I think about him, the more I realize he didn't look too happy about his reservation being confirmed. In fact, he looked like the idea of having dinner with his date was nothing more than a chore.

I don't think I will ever understand guys like Christian. I mean why go on a date if you don't want to? If he's only interested in a hook up, why doesn't he join Tinder or something where everyone is in the same boat? A good looking guy like him would have no trouble finding someone to spend the night with.

I shrug my shoulders. Christian and his strange behavior when it comes to dating really isn't my concern. What is my concern is getting the last of these files digitized like I have been asked to do.

CHRISTIAN

As I walk towards the conference room, my mind is once more on Ava. Did I see a flicker of disappointment on her face when she told me she had secured my reservation for later this evening? I mean she must know it's a date – it's that kind of place, plus if I was meeting with a client, I would have had her contact them too partly as a common courtesy and partly to confirm the booking.

So ok, she knows it's a date. But why would she care? And why do I care whether or not she cares anyway? Yeah, she doesn't care. I imagined that look on her face. Maybe I wanted her to be disappointed. No, that's stupid. There's no denying the girl is stunning, but it doesn't change the fact she's far too uptight for me. I don't want her to be disappointed. I don't want her to be anything except my secretary. Except... no, stop it right now, I tell myself. Think about something else. Anything else.

With a huge effort, I shake away my thoughts of Ava as I reach the conference room. I can't afford to be distracted in my first partner's meeting, and besides, I don't need to keep thinking about Ava. She's a good legal secretary and that's all I need her to be. See, I can do this.

I step into the room. It's already quite full but I'm not the last to arrive. Matthew nods at me and I return the gesture. It's weird thinking of Mr. Foley as Matthew after growing up calling him Mr. Foley, but like he pointed out, we're on level ground now and the partners would think it was weird if I called him Mr. Foley and he called me Christian.

By the time the last couple of partners arrive in the conference room, I've made myself a cup of coffee and I'm sitting down beside Matthew at the head of the table.

"Right, let's get started," Matthew says when the last few stragglers have grabbed refreshments and taken their seats.

There's a bit of shuffling around and the sound of papers being reorganized, but the chatter in the room dies down pretty much instantly and all eyes are on us.

"Thank you all for joining us," Matthew says with a warm smile. "The first thing on this evening's agenda is for us to officially welcome Christian as our new managing partner. I'm sure a lot of you have already met him, but it's always nice to do things officially."

Matthew begins to clap and everyone joins in. I smile around at everyone, feeling a little bit awkward. I am relieved when the applause stops and Matthew moves on from me.

"Ok. The second thing on the agenda is the Wilson case. How's that going? Macey? Dan?" Matthew says, looking down at his notes and then back up at the partners, his gaze sitting on Macey and Dan.

Macey and Dan take it in turns to feed us the information about the case they are working on, each of them filling in the gaps with their individual expertise. The case seems to be progressing nicely and Macey has found some irregularities in the books of the opposition which in theory, should win us the case. She's good. She's looked where most people wouldn't even think to look.

Matthew praises her and Dan and then he moves around the room, getting updates from the partners on all of the big cases and any new clients. Overall, things are going well and I'm pleased with the results we're getting. Matthew seems to be equally pleased and the meeting has a nice feel to it, unlike some of the meetings I've been in at my past firms where the managing partners have ranted and raved and ripped everyone new ones.

After we go through all of the cases and their updates, talk moves onto which junior partners are smashing it and which of them might be the next to be offered a senior partnership. The debate gets quite heated as all of the partners fight for the junior partners who started out as their associates, and if I'm honest, I tune out a bit. I don't know any of these people enough to have any sort of an input, and the next partnership won't open up for another three months anyway so I really can't see the point in having this argument so early. Anything could happen in the next three months and then we'll have to have it all out all over again.

My ears prick up slightly when someone suggests Gary Prewitt. I've only been here for a short amount of time and even I know that would be a bad idea. I am relieved when Matthew and several of the other partners shoot the idea down straight away so that I don't have to. I have no problem stating my opinion, but with me being so new, I know it would cause tension if I vetoed someone everyone else was happy with.

The man is useless. I honestly don't know how he got a law degree, let alone a junior partnership here. I have paralegals who know far more about the law than he does. Fucking hell, Ava is only a legal secretary and even she knows more about the law than he does – I'd send her to court on behalf of one of my clients before I sent Gary Prewitt that's for sure.

And just like that, I am completely tuned out of the partnership debate and my mind is firmly back on Ava. I know that thinking about her is dangerous ground and I should force myself to think about something else, force myself to pay attention to the next discussion that's happening around the table, but I don't. I let the thoughts of Ava come to me, her image playing across my mind.

I see her sitting at her desk, looking up as my office door opens, peering at me from beneath her long, dark eyelashes. I see her smile, her eyes twinkling as they crinkle ever so slightly at the corners. I see how damned good she looks in a pencil skirt and a fitted blouse, showing off her curves while staying perfectly demure and somehow making me want to rip the blouse off of her and shove that skirt up over her hips and fuck her.

I see her in my bed, her orgasm fading, leaving her cheeks red, her skin glowing, her chest heaving. I see the sated look in her eyes that is quickly replaced by a hungry look as she pushes me onto my back and straddles me.

I shift slightly in my seat, feeling myself blushing as I come back to my senses and remind myself that I'm in a room full

77

of people. I clear my throat and take a sip from a glass of water that sits in front of me. I must be doing a reasonable job of appearing to be normal because no one is looking at me. They are still debating something although I have completely lost track of what it is now.

"Anything to add?" Matthew says to me, startling me slightly.

I shake my head mutely and then I recover my composure slightly and speak up. "Not at this time. It's my belief that the right candidate for partnership could still come forward and prove themselves between now and three months' time," I say, sending up a silent prayer that they are still talking about partnership.

"Yes, that's true," Matthew says, nodding his approval.

I breathe a metaphorical sigh of relief that I have managed to provide an answer that made sense to the situation. A few of the partners around the room are also nodding their heads in agreement with my point. A few scowl too but no one voices any counter argument.

"Right then, this meeting is adjourned," Matthew adds with a smile.

Everyone begins to talk at once as chairs scrape back and people start to head for the conference room doors. I'm a little bit shocked that the meeting is over so quickly. I shrug. I'm not complaining about it – I hate how these things usually drag on for hours. I stand up and check my watch and my eyes widen in surprise. It seems the meeting wasn't over quickly at all, more that my mind wandered enough that I lost track of the time. It's almost nine thirty.

I guess I've stood Natalie up then. I feel a small stab of guilt, but it's over before it really consumes me. The truth is, what I really feel is relief that I don't have to go on this date to make my father think I'm following his instructions to settle down. And he can't complain about this one because if he tries to, every senior partner at the firm and Matthew can confirm that I was in a partner meeting. My father might want me to settle down and not have the firm consume my whole life, but even he would be forced to agree that the partner meeting was more important than a date.

I leave the conference room and start back towards my office calling my goodbyes to the others as I go. I debate calling Natalie, but what's the point? Either she'll ignore my call, or she'll take it and yell at me and I can do without that to be honest. The best case scenario is she takes my call, forgives me, and we rearrange another date I don't want to go on.

It's funny that I always had a thing for Natalie until there was a chance for us and now, I don't know, I guess she just doesn't hold the same appeal to me. And it's not her. Objectively, I know she's one hell of a woman and I'm mentally kicking myself for not going out with her, but something has changed and it's been different for a while now. Since I started working here in fact.

I think my father trying to force me into some sort of relationship has put me off the idea altogether. It has to be that. It can't possibly be that whenever I think of going out with someone, I compare them to Ava and they always come up short.

No, of course it's not that. That would be ludicrous. Ava is needy and uptight and so not my type at all, and even if she were my type, I don't want to get all serious and settle down. I want to…

The thought dies on me when I round the corner into the corridor leading to my office and see Ava still sitting there at her desk. She's peering intently at her computer monitor, her fingers dancing over the keyboard. Her hair is pinned back, but one tendril has come loose and she blows it gently off her face. She is a vision, there's no denying that. And there's no denying the rush of lust I feel when she looks up from the monitor, catches my eye and flashes me that smile of hers.

AVA

I've gotten through quite a few of the files I am digitizing. As soon as the office mostly cleared out and all was quiet, including the telephone, I was able to really focus and get through each file much quicker than I can during the day when I have everything else to do as well. I want to get a few more done before I stop though. It's not that late yet and the sooner these are done, the better.

I can feel a strand of hair tickling my face and I blow it absently away as I keep typing. I slowly become aware of a feeling inside of me like I'm being watched. I glance up from the screen, not really expecting to see anyone there, but I find myself looking into Christian's eyes.

I gasp slightly and I hope the sound didn't carry to Christian. I flash him a quick smile and then look back at my monitor. I turn slightly and my elbow catches the file I'm working on and it falls to the floor.

I jump off my chair and get on my knees, gathering up the fallen papers. I can feel my face blushing with embarrassment. Of all the times for that to happen, it couldn't have happened while I was alone. I'm more than a little bit flustered by the time I've retrieved all of the sheets, but I am so grateful that they are at least numbered so I can get them back in the right order easily enough.

As I push the papers into the file they fell from, I happen to glance at my watch and my jaw drops. How the hell is it after nine already? I must have been way more engrossed in my work than I even realized. But why is Christian here at this time? He should be at the restaurant now.

Dread fills my stomach as I stand back up. I must have messed up the reservation and Christian has come back to fire me for it. I will be upset with myself if I have made such a silly mistake, but I won't let him bully me. He's not going to get to fire me for something that isn't even work related.

I tilt my chin up slightly, holding my head up high. Christian is almost at my desk. He takes another couple of steps until he reaches it and then he perches on it and smiles at me, shaking his head.

"What on earth are you still doing here Ava?" he asks.

His tone throws me even more than his question. He doesn't sound angry at all. I'm not quite ready to let my guard down just yet though. I nod to the pile of files on my desk.

"I wanted to get through a few of these while it was quiet," I say. Christian doesn't speak, he just looks at me. I can feel myself squirming under his gaze, a combination of lust and panic. He doesn't look mad though. Still, he could just be hiding it, biding his time to yell at me. I have to know if I'm about to get raked over the coals for some sort of fuck up with the restaurant, and before I can change my mind, I blurt it out. "Why aren't you at the restaurant?"

"The partner meeting ran over," Christian says. "It just finished. I was just coming to grab my jacket and then I'm going to the diner across the street for some dinner. Would you like to join me?"

I'm more than a little bit taken aback by Christian's offer, and if I'm honest, I'm more than a little bit pissed off too. His date fell through so I'm his second choice? I don't think so. I don't want an argument either so I go with what I think is a safe enough refusal.

"I'm still finishing up here, maybe some other time though," I say.

"Oh come on, it's far too late to be worrying about a few files," Christian says.

I open my mouth to tell him I'm not really hungry, but of course my stomach chooses that exact moment to growl.

"See. You know you want to," Christian grins. He digs in his pocket for a moment, the grin on his face turning mischievous as he holds up his company credit card. "Come on, call it a bonus."

I sigh and nod my head, resigned to the fact that I am doing this.

"Ok," I say quietly.

I suppose if Christian is willing to make the effort for us to be friends, I should be willing to at least try to do the same. And it's not like I'm his second choice date because this isn't a date. Not at all. It's just two colleagues grabbing dinner together rather than both eating alone because normal people have already eaten by now.

The second choice thing still stings a little bit though, even though I try to tell myself its stupid. If this same scenario had occurred with anyone else in the office, I wouldn't feel pissed off. So why do I feel pissed off with Christian? I mean I don't even like him so why would I care that I am his second best option?

CHRISTIAN

I watch Ava as she blows gently on the surface of her coffee.

"Are you sure you wouldn't rather have a cocktail?" I ask her. "I can drive you home."

"No honestly this is fine," Ava smiles, nodding down at her coffee. She rubs a hand across her belly and shakes her head and laughs. "I'm so full I need the coffee to settle everything."

"Yeah you were definitely right about those burgers," I laugh.

Ava had tried to convince me to get a normal burger, but I had insisted we have the tower burgers and my God where they huge. I don't know how we even got through them but we did. I know what Ava means about being so full now though. And she's right about the coffee as well - it is definitely helping me to feel less stuffed so I take another sip.

I should probably be a bit miffed that I missed out on a gourmet three course meal in a fancy restaurant and had a burger in a diner instead, but here's the thing – I'm not at all.

85

I much prefer normal food to the over-priced fancy stuff they serve in those places where you spend a hundred dollars on a meal and come out still feeling hungry. And as much as I hate to admit it, Ava and I have had a good time together with plenty of laughter. In truth, I think she's probably better company than Natalie would have been and it will certainly be less awkward at the end of the night saying see you tomorrow to Ava than it would be saying see you again never to Natalie.

"They were good, but far too big," Ava says. "I'm honestly still shocked I finished all of mine."

"That'll cost you at least an extra hour in the gym," I grin.

Ava frowns and shakes her head. She looks at me, her face contorted with anger.

"Are you trying to say I'm fat?" she demands.

"What? No. Of course not. I was just joking," I say quickly, horrified that she thinks I'm saying she's fat.

She bursts into laughter.

"Got you," she says.

When my laugh joins hers, it's partly because yeah that was genuinely funny, and it's also partly because I'm filled with relief when I realize that she's joking and that she doesn't really think I was insulting her. When the laughter fades, I find myself watching Ava, appreciating the sparkle in her eyes and the way her hair shines in the glare of the neon light above us.

"You know, I'm kind of glad I missed my date tonight," I confess. "I don't think the food would have been this good. Or the company."

Ava shakes her head but she's smiling. I get the impression my comment has pleased her, even though she's trying to hide that fact from me.

"It might be best not to mention that when you do go on your date," she says.

"What do you mean?" I frown. "I can't see Natalie giving me a second chance after I stood her up tonight."

"You didn't call her?" Ava says, a look of horror on her face.

"I lost track of the time," I say with a shrug. "And by the time the meeting finished it was so late it didn't seem worth calling her then just to get yelled at."

"Oh well," Ava says. "Next time you run into her, just pretend like you don't know her. Because that won't be awkward at all."

The slight flush of Ava's cheeks alongside her words tells me everything I need to know about where she came up with that idea. Fuck.

"Ava. I …" I start but she shakes her head and cuts me off.

"Relax," she says. "Honestly, I'm over it. I just wanted to see your reaction."

"You didn't exactly rush to greet me like a long-lost friend," I point out.

"True," Ava says. "But you were pretending not to know me. There was no way I was risking you keep rolling with that and me looking like a crazy person in front of your dad."

"Fair enough," I say.

I pick my coffee up and take a drink, wishing I could think of something to say that would change the subject without it being obvious that was what I was trying to do. I fail miserably. I look down into my cup but I look up again when Ava laughs softly.

"Honestly, it's fine. I shouldn't have brought it up. I know it wasn't really about me. Just like the way you acted the next morning after we… well you know," Ava says. "It was definitely more about you than me."

"What do you mean by that?" I ask with a raised eyebrow.

"Oh I just mean your fear of commitment," she says. "The way you made sure I wouldn't want to see you ever again the morning after our night together. The way you purposely arranged a date the same night as the partner meeting knowing the meeting was likely to run over and you wouldn't make the reservation."

I shake my head and frown at Ava.

"You think you know me, but you don't know the first thing about any of this," I say.

"Ok," she says.

She smiles and that's somehow more infuriating than it would have been if she had argued.

"It's just… things are complicated right now, that's all," I say.

"Ok," Ava says again with that same infuriating smile.

I'm done being analyzed like this, and now I'm remembering why I thought being friendly with Ava could be a mistake. I down the last of my coffee and motion to our waitress for the check. Ava finishes the last of her coffee too. She puts the cup down and stands up.

"I'm just going to the ladies' room," she says.

I nod and watch her as she walks away towards the facilities at the back of the diner. I can't help but keep my eyes on her. It's the way her black pencil skirt clings to her hips and accentuates her perfect little ass. It's the way her hips sway ever so slightly as she moves, and the way her hair swings slightly with each step.

I'm pulled out of my thoughts of running my hands over that perfect little ass when our waitress puts the check down on the table.

"Thanks," I smile.

I check it and leave enough to cover the bill plus the tip and then I stand up and head for the door. I debate just leaving rather than having to see Ava's smug look as she tells me all about how I'm afraid of commitment, but of course I know I can't do that. We might be just across the street from the office, but I'm not going to risk anything happening to her by leaving her to walk the streets alone at night.

To be honest, I don't even know why she's pissing me off so much with her assumption. The way I acted when we spent the night together certainly would have given anyone the impression I don't want a relationship and I suppose I wasn't exactly acting like serious boyfriend material with Natalie either. I think the main reason she's pissing me off is because she keeps saying I'm afraid to commit. That's not true at all. I'm not afraid, I'm just happy playing the field. If she had said she thinks my behavior is because I don't want to commit, I could probably have happily accepted that.

After a few seconds, Ava comes back from the bathroom. She doesn't give me a smug look, she just smiles at me, her normal smile and I smile back. I'm still annoyed with her, but I don't really want an argument here. I tell myself it really doesn't matter what Ava thinks anyway.

I open the door of the diner and gesture for Ava to step through. She smiles and thanks me as she steps outside. I expect the cold evening air to sting my face after the warmth of the diner, but it's cool rather than cold and the breeze is surprisingly nice on my skin.

"I'm really not afraid of commitment you know," I say as we wait to cross the street.

"You don't need to explain yourself to me Christian," Ava replies as we see a gap in the traffic and cross the street and head for our building.

She's right. I don't need to explain myself to her or anyone else for that matter, but I still feel like I want to. I don't know why, but for some reason, I don't want Ava to think badly of me.

"I know, but I'm just saying it's not true, that's all," I say.

We've reached the entrance to our offices and Ava pauses. For a second, I think she's going to enter the building, but instead, she puts her hand on my arm, stopping me too.

"I'm sorry. I shouldn't have said anything," she says. "I have this thing where my mouth tends to pop into gear before my brain and…"

She's still talking but I'm no longer listening. I am mesmerized by her at this moment. By the way she's trying to make things right between us, by the expression on her face, and most of all, by that hand on my arm that sends shivers through my body and reminds me what it feels like to have this girl in my arms.

Before I have had a chance to think it through or stop myself, I lean down and press my lips against Ava's, cutting her off mid sentence. For a second, she stiffens, but then she melts into my kiss and she starts kissing me back, her arms going around my waist.

I push one hand into her hair and walk her backwards until she's leaning against the building. I put my other hand on the wall by her head as she squirms her body against mine. I can feel my desire for Ava overtaking all of my senses, but I manage to keep my head enough to not start undressing her, as much as I might want to.

After a few delicious, torturous moments, I pull my lips back from Ava's, knowing that if I don't, I'm not going to be able to stop myself from hitching her skirt up and fucking the life out of her right here in the street. We stand there, my hand moving from her hair and caressing her cheek, my other hand still in place on the wall. Ava's arms are still around me as we look into each other's eyes.

I feel as though I can hardly breathe, like I can hardly think. Ava is consuming me completely. Her chest heaves as she pants for breath and I think she might feel the same way about me in this moment as I do about her. I'm certain of it when she wriggles free and takes my hand in hers, leading me towards the parking lot and over to her car. She unlocks it as we're almost there and nods to the passenger door.

"Get in," she says.

Her voice is thick and husky and I feel a pang of desire flood through me at the sound of it. I don't hesitate to follow her command – because that's what it is, a command, not a request – and I get into the passenger seat of her car. She must want me to go back to her place instead of the other way around, or else she wants her own car at mine for the morning. Whatever she wants she can have right now.

The driver's door opens and Ava gets into the car, but she doesn't slip in on her ass ready to drive. She gets in on her knees, and before I have a chance to even wonder what she's doing, her skirt is up around her hips and she's straddling me on the passenger seat.

I can feel the heat coming off her pussy even through my pants and I moan as Ava tugs my shirt free of them and runs her hands over my skin. She pulls her hands away and begins to unbutton my shirt, leaning in and brushing her lips against mine as she does it.

I reach for her, holding her in place when she goes to dart back from my lips. She surrenders to me, slipping her tongue into my mouth and kissing me with a desperate longing that matches the way I feel deep inside. I meet her tongue with mine, caressing hers. She pushes my jacket and shirt down my arms and I work with her, shaking the cuffs loose from my wrists, leaving me bare from the waist up.

It's my turn now and I fumble the buttons of Ava's blouse open and push it open. I put my hands on her sides and then move them to her back, rubbing them all over her skin, wanting to feel every inch of her. I can't help but notice she isn't wearing a bra and I move my lips from hers and kiss down her throat and chest until I reach her bare breasts with my mouth.

I suck on her nipples, one after the other, bringing them to points, making Ava moan as I nibble lightly on one of them. I rest one hand on her hip and the other hand, I pull out from beneath her blouse and rub it across the silky smooth dampness of her panties. I feel her gasp in a breath, her chest jerking against me as I tease her, my touch barely there.

She presses down, pressing herself onto my fingers and as I begin to massage her clit, she moves her hips in a circle, working with me to bring her right to the edge. As I work Ava's clit, I kiss my way back up her chest and find her lips with my own again.

I kiss her, revelling in the taste of her, the smell of her. I need to touch her properly and I slip my fingers inside of her panties, touching her already swollen clit directly. She stiffens slightly and moans into my mouth as my fingers move across her clit, bringing her to life.

I press harder, moving my fingers faster. She pulls her lips from mine and presses her face into the side of my neck as her orgasm takes her. I feel her body stiffen, feel the heat of her gasped breaths on my neck and the sticky, warm juices coating my fingers as she comes hard.

I slip my fingers back out of her panties and unbutton my pants. I need to be inside of her, need to feel her tight little pussy wrapped around me. And I need it now. I need to feel how slick and slippery she is, how ready for me her body is.

I lift my ass up and pull my pants and boxer shorts down slightly. I return my ass to the seat and take Ava by her hip with one hand. I use my other hand to push her panties to one side, exposing her pussy. I can feel her panting against my neck, still reeling from her orgasm, but I can't wait any longer so she gets no reprieve. I hold her still and slam into her, filling her up, her wet heat wrapping around me.

She makes an ah sound and lifts her head up away from my shoulder, looking at me through lust heavy eyes. She arches her back and throws her head back as I start to thrust into her and she moves up and down in time with me, coating me in her juices, rubbing herself over the full length of my cock.

I want this to last forever, but no matter how much my head screams at me to slow down, to make it last, my body doesn't listen. Before I know it, I'm slamming into Ava faster and faster and as she climaxes once more, her pussy tightening even further around my cock, I can't stop my own orgasm from taking over me.

My whole body feels the intense rush of pleasure that starts in my cock and spreads up into my stomach and all of the way through me. My cock is going wild inside of Ava, twitching and spasming as I spurt into her.

I try to snatch a breath but I can't get any air. It's like my body is frozen, held in place by the intensity of the orgasm I'm having. I have never felt anything quite like this in my life. All too soon though, it's over and I slip out of Ava.

I'm finally able to breathe and I wrap my arms around Ava as she collapses against me, her head on my shoulder. I watch her move up and down in time with my chest as I fight to get myself back under control.

Finally, my breathing evens out, but Ava is making no move to get off my lap and I'm more than content to sit here and hold her in my arms. This encounter has made me remember just how much fun Ava can be when she lets loose and stops being uptight. In fact, sitting here with Ava in my arms, her juices still drying on my cock, I can hardly remember why I didn't want to see her again after the last time.

After a few minutes, Ava pushes herself up from me a bit. She smiles at me and rubs her lips gently over mine. Even this feather light touch is enough to get my pulse racing once more as my desire for her courses through my body. Ava's kiss deepens, becoming more passionate and my hands roam her body as I kiss her back.

She pulls back from the kiss, a teasing smile on her face. She raises an eyebrow and glances down at my cock which is once again rock hard.

"Someone's eager," she says.

"Your fault," I smile.

She laughs softly and leans in and kisses me again. The kiss is shorter, barely a touch, and then she's kissing down my neck and down my chest. She shuffles her legs around and within seconds, she's no longer straddling me; she's kneeling on the floorboard between my feet. She leans her head forward and I gasp as she sucks my cock into her mouth.

She holds the base of it in her fist as she licks up and down my length, licking me clean of her juices. She moans and makes "mmm" sounds as she goes. The sounds of her enjoying the taste of me sends shocks of pleasure flooding through me, and I feel myself getting harder in her mouth as desire overcomes me.

Her hands are on my thighs and as her sucking gets more intense, I can't help but move my hips in time with her head and as I do, my thighs move beneath her palms, sending shivers up into my already pulsing cock.

I know I'm not going to be able to hold myself back any longer and I rest my head back against the seat with my eyes screwed tightly closed, and I ball my hands into fists as my orgasm slams through me and I spurt into Ava's mouth. She keeps sucking even as I spurt, swallowing my seed and keeps sucking until I spurt again. I feel like she's trying to suck me dry and it feels fucking amazing. My orgasm seems to last forever as Ava keeps on working on my cock.

When it finally fades, I slip out of her mouth. I lift my head back up and open my eyes and look down at Ava. She looks amazing on her knees down there, looking up at me, her hair mussed up and her lipstick smeared. Her cheeks are flushed and she smiles at me. I return her smile.

She reaches up to her face and wipes away a smear of spunk I hadn't noticed from her chin. She then puts her fingers in her mouth and sucks them clean, all while looking me straight in the eye. I feel myself tingling once more as I watch her sucking and licking her fingers and I want nothing more than to take her home and never let her go.

She reaches her hands up to me and I take them and support her while she slides up from the floorboard and straddles me again. She leans down and kisses me full on the lips and then she pushes herself away, sliding back into the driver's seat of her car.

"Well, goodnight then Christian," she says in a low, husky voice. "Thank you for dinner."

For a second, I'm not sure how to respond to that and I just look at her. She looks back at me, a patient smile on her face as she puts her key in the ignition and sets the engine running. I realize what's happening. She's dismissing me.

"Umm, see you tomorrow," I say, quickly fastening my trousers and groping around for my shirt.

I pull it on and get out of the car without fastening it, slinging my jacket over my arm. I walk towards my car, barely feeling the cold night air on my bare chest. I turn to wave at Ava as her engine roars to life, but she's already gone past me without so much as a backwards glance.

I feel my lips curling up into a smile. She knows exactly what she's doing, that girl. She's playing me at my own game, and I hate to admit it, but I think she's winning. Because suddenly I'm longing for more of her, and as I get into my car, all I can think about is when we're going to be able to do that again.

CHRISTIAN

My mind is on Ava as I sit in my office waiting for my father to arrive. It seems like my mind is constantly on Ava these days. I should be used to it by now I guess but I'm not. It's new and exciting and yeah, I quite like it.

I got in to work early on purpose this morning. As I was showering and getting dressed, I kept telling myself I wanted to be in early so I could get prepared for my meeting with my father. The truth is, I have no idea what my father wants to talk to me about so it's not like I could prepare for it. He just called me this morning and said he'd be coming in to see me early this morning. He sounded happy though so that's good.

The real reason I wanted to be in nice and early was so that I could get in before Ava. It's not that I'm avoiding her as such, I just think I'll be more comfortable if I'm in my office when I first see her again after last night rather than being able to feel her eyes upon me as I walk along the corridor to my office.

I don't know what to do for the best at this point, whether to talk to Ava about what happened between us last night or not? I keep trying to tell myself that I only want to talk to her about it to make sure that there's no hard feelings or anything now that we're working together, but the truth is, I really think I want to ask her out. I can't get her out of my head. She's all I've thought about from leaving her car to falling asleep last night, and she's all I've thought about since I woke up this morning right through right now. And I have a feeling she's going to be all I can think about for quite some time to come now.

I look up as there's a knock at my office door. Is it her? I run my hands through my hair and straighten my tie, just in case it is her.

"Come in," I shout.

The door opens and of course it's not her, it's my father. I stand up and go to greet him, smiling at him. He shakes my hand and then pulls me in for a quick hug before releasing me and smiling widely at me. We head to the seating area as I frown across at him. Something is going on. He's still smiling that smile, like an excited child.

"What brings you here today then?" I ask once we're seated.

"Oh come on Christian don't play shy with me," he says. "Isn't there something you want to tell me?"

Is there something I want to tell him? Or even something I maybe don't particularly want to tell him but that he would want to know? No, not that I can think of. I mean surely he doesn't mean the Jackson and Lowe merger. There was never any doubt I was going to win that case. It's the only thing I can think of though and so with a shrug, I tell him about that.

"We got Gerald Jackson the deal he wanted on the Jackson and Lowe merger," I say.

"I should think so," my father says. "An associate could have gotten that deal to go through."

Ok, so it wasn't that then.

"Try again," my father grins, not seeming to be in the least bit disheartened by the fact I have no idea what he's talking about.

"I'm sorry. I have absolutely no idea what you're talking about," I say after a moment, hoping that my bluntness will get him to help me out a bit here.

I'm only pleased he looks happy at this point. If I have done something impressive I've forgotten about, I can live with that. If I've fucked something up and forgotten about it, then I would be ashamed of myself.

"Ava," my father says.

Except of course he didn't say Ava. He can't have. Why would he be asking me about Ava? Wow, she really is consuming my thoughts today.

"What?" I say.

"Ava," my father says again. This time, I have no doubt that I heard him correctly.

"What… what about her?" I say, frowning at him.

He throws his head back and laughs. I smile self-consciously, not sure how to react to the laughter.

"You don't have to pretend for my sake Christian. I'm not angry. In fact, I couldn't be happier for the two of you," he says.

I'm starting to get a bit annoyed now. It must be obvious to him that I have absolutely no idea what he's talking about and yet he's still looking at me expectantly. I sigh.

"Look I'm sorry but I still have no idea what you're talking about," I tell him.

He rolls his eyes but he's still smiling.

"I really thought I would have gotten it out of you without me having to tell you what I saw, but here we are," my father says. "You know the CCTV cameras for this place feedback to my home computer still, right? And I still tend to keep an eye on them when the building is mostly deserted."

"No, I had no idea you could see the CCTV, but that doesn't clear things up any," I say, trying to buy myself some time. Oh, what's the point! He must know I know what he means at this point.

I feel the heat rush to my cheeks. If he didn't know I knew what he was talking about before, he sure as hell does now, but I can't help it. I don't know what's worse. That my father saw Ava and me having sex in her car, or the fact that he's laughing about it. I just want to die on the spot, but obviously, that's not an option.

"I'm sorry, we just got a bit carried away," I say. "It won't happen again, I swear."

My father's laughter fades slightly and he narrows his eyes at me slanting his head to one side like he always does when he's pondering something.

"God Christian, relax. It was only a kiss goodnight for goodness sake. I didn't think you would be embarrassed by me seeing you two kissing. But just so you know, if you're that worried about who can see you kissing, then kissing in the main street like that probably isn't a good idea," he says.

Relief floods me when I realize he only saw Ava and me kissing at the front of the building. He didn't see what happened once we got into the parking lot. I think for a moment, trying to come up with something plausible that will cover my complete over reaction to the thought of my dad seeing me kiss someone.

"I just don't want to get Ava into any trouble that's all," I say. "You know, dating in the office, that kind of thing."

My father waves his hand, waving away my words.

"I don't care about any of that and I know Matthew doesn't either. Unless of course it starts affecting either of your work," he says. "I'm so happy for you, son. You couldn't have chosen a better girl."

This is my moment to tell my father that it was just one kiss. That we're not together or anything like that. I open my mouth to tell him, but he's still talking.

"While you and Ava are together, you can relax son. There's no way I'll be handing off my half of the company to Lewis Foley; not when you and Ava can do so much good together and really make this company huge again," he says.

Again, I know this is the moment to tell him that Ava and I aren't even together. He looks so happy, and I know telling him this is only going to piss him off, but surely it will piss him off even more if I don't tell him until later. The thing is though, I don't want to risk what's rightfully mine going to Lewis Foley, but it's more than that. In this moment, I can see that my father is proud of me, and I don't want that to turn to anger. So instead of taking my chance to tell him he's gotten it all wrong, I smile instead.

"I really like her Dad," I say. It's not a lie. Not really. I mean I do quite like her when she's not being clingy and uptight. "But it's in the early days yet so please don't go getting too carried away ok."

"I'm not getting carried away. I just said I'm happy for you that's all," my father says.

"Good," I say. "Because no one in here really knows about us and we're trying to keep things fairly quiet for now with it being so new."

"Well I'm sure Matthew won't be in a hurry to tell people," my dad replies.

"You told Matthew? What the fuck dad," I say.

"No, of course I didn't," he says. "Do Matthew and I seem like the type to sit gossiping?"

"Well no," I admit. "So how does he know?"

God was he watching the CCTV footage too?

"He doesn't yet unless of course you two aren't as discrete as you think you are. But he'll obviously work it out when he sees Ava is your date for the charity gala this weekend," he says.

"Oh, of course, I forgot about that. I don't think I'll be bringing Ava. Like I say, it's all pretty new and that gala is a big deal for you and Mom," I say.

"Well it is, and normally I would agree with you, but it's not like Ava is a stranger. She's not going to show you or us up at the gala," my father says. I open my mouth to give him some other objection, but he shakes his head before I even start. "I won't take no for an answer."

"Well then I guess we'll see you Saturday then," I say with a forced smile.

"Indeed," my father replies.

He gets up and makes his way towards my office door. I'm shocked to hear that he's whistling. He reaches the door and pulls it open and then he turns back to me. He looks happier than I've seen him in years.

"Your mom is going to be so pleased about this," he says. "You know how she worries. This will be a big weight off her mind."

With that, he's gone before I can reply. But if I could have replied, what is there to say? By Saturday, I'm going to pretty much break my mom's heart and piss my father right off. But what can I do? I can hardly invite Ava to the gala as a friend and just hope no one says anything off to her.

No, I'll have to just go to the gala alone and tell my parents that Ava and I broke up. Unless…. no, that's a bad idea. Or is it? I know if I go through with the idea, there's no way Ava and I can have another session together like last night. But I also know if I don't go through with the idea, my parents will be on my case constantly about settling down, and Lewis fucking Foley will be one step closer to getting his grubby little hands on my half of this company.

I'm not going to let this happen. I'm going to have to go ahead with the plan and just hope I can convince Ava it's a good idea. And then I'm going to have to let go of the idea of us going on a date or having sex or kissing or anything ever again.

AVA

As I drove out of that parking lot last night without so much as glancing back at Christian, I felt so empowered. It was like a major adrenaline rush, knowing I had surprised Christian and left him wanting more, and all of the way home, I felt like I could do anything. I went into my apartment like I was walking on air. I got into bed and fell asleep quickly, a contented smile on my face.

I woke up this morning and everything felt different again. I keep saying I'm not a one night stand kind of a girl, and to be fair, the last time Christian and I slept together, I had no way of knowing he only wanted that one night with me. But this time, I know him and I know he's not one for commitment. I knew when we kissed last night that if I let it go any further, it would be a one night stand. And I didn't just let it go further, I took control and pushed it further myself.

Does that mean I am a one night stand kind of a girl? I don't know. I still don't think of myself that way. Like I wouldn't go to a club just looking to hook up for a night, or anything like that. But when the opportunity presents itself, I don't exactly say no thank you either. So who knows? Maybe the lesson here is that I shouldn't put labels on stuff, I should just take things how they come and roll with the punches so to speak.

Ok, that's one less thing to worry about, but it's far from the only thing I've been worrying about. In fact, it's the least important thing and I have been using it to keep my mind off the important thing. I have no idea how it's going to go with Christian. Are we going to have an awkward conversation about it? Are we going to pretend like it didn't happen? I don't know and I don't like not knowing things. I like being able to plan in advance for situations that are going to likely be awkward. And this is definitely one of those situations.

I sit at my kitchen table long after the coffee in front of me has gone cold. I hate being late for work, and if I am late today, it's going to look like I'm taking liberties, but I just can't face sitting at my desk and having to watch Christian walk the length of the hallway wondering what he's going to say or do when he reaches me.

I picture it, me sitting there, cringing inside. Him coming towards me. I stand up as he reaches my desk and start to apologize. He tells me not to apologize and before I can say anything else, he has his hands cupping my face, his lips on mine. It seems so real, my imagination bringing everything to life so vividly, that for a moment, I can almost feel Christian's kiss.

I shake my head, shaking away the image. I'm almost certain that won't happen and sitting here imagining it will is doing nothing to make me feel more relaxed about the situation. I struggle to let go of the image completely, and then when I do, I find it replaced by an image of our real kiss last night, me pressed up against the building, Christian's lips on mine, his tongue in my mouth. His kiss was so passionate, so hot, I had felt myself melting into him, powerless to stop him even if I had wanted to.

It's funny that our kiss seemed to happen mostly because Christian wanted to shut me up. I mean I know at times I piss him off a bit because I tell him the honest truths no one else will I suspect, but I wasn't expecting that to be the outcome of it. If I had known pissing Christian off could get him to kiss me like that, I might have pissed him off much more and much sooner.

Maybe being late today will turn out to be a good thing. Not because it will take away any awkwardness between us, but because it will piss Christian off and maybe I'll get another kiss like that one. And then maybe he'll lift me up and swipe his desk clean, sitting me on the edge of it, my skirt around my hips. And then he'll tear my panties off me, throw them away and fuck me senseless.

Fucking hell, what's going on with me? I've just been telling myself I'm not that kind of girl, and already I'm fantasizing about the next time Christian and I fuck. There isn't going to be a next time though. This is awkward enough. Christian won't commit and I'm certainly not being one of those friends with benefits types who is basically being used and can't even see it. I still have a modicum of self-respect left and I intend to keep it that way.

I'm still no further forward on how to handle this, and I don't want to give Christian all the power by just waiting for him to act or not act. I need some sort of a game plan. I decide to call Sophie. She'll know how to play it. I pick my cell phone up and call her. She answers quickly with a whispered hang on. I remember she had her date with Mr Surfer Type last night and I'm guessing the whispering means she's still with him. I wouldn't have called if I had remembered sooner, but she's taken my call so she can't be mad at me for calling.

"Hey what's up," she says at a normal volume a moment or two later.

"You first," I say. "How did your date go?"

"Perfect," Sophie gushes. "We came back to his place last night and I'm sure you can guess what we did. Then this morning we've had breakfast and we're going to spend the morning together and then go for lunch somewhere nice."

"Wow," I say. "Sounds like you two are really into each other."

"I don't want to jinx things, but yeah, we are," she says. "Now spill. You don't call me this early unless something is wrong."

"It's not wrong exactly. It's... awkward I guess. Remember the last time we were out and I told you I went home with that guy?" I say.

"Mr. Hot But Not, yeah I remember," Sophie says.

"Well, it turns out he was my boss's son and when my boss took early retirement, guess who got his job," I say.

"Noooo," Sophie says, the shock in her voice clear to hear. "And you're just telling me this now? Your boss retired weeks ago."

"Yeah it wasn't that big of a deal," I reply. "Until we slept together again last night."

"What?" Sophie shouts so loud I have to move the cell phone from my ear slightly. I hear a male voice in the background.

"Two seconds," Sophie says to me and then louder. "It's my best friend, Ava. She's screwing her boss and she needs advice. I won't be long."

"Jeez Soph, do you have to?" I say.

"Oh relax. It's not like he knows either of you. Now, where were we? Oh yes. You had sex again last night. So are you guys like dating now?"

"No," I say. "Christian isn't the commitment type. And to be honest, he's not really my type either."

"Good looking. Good in bed. Very good job and salary. Yeah I can see why he wouldn't be your type," Sophie says.

"He's an arrogant jerk at times," I say, but the argument sounds weak, even to me, and with horror, I wonder if it's possible that I'm actually starting to like Christian. "But that's not the point. The point is, I don't know how to act around him now. Do I bring up last night? Do I act like nothing happened? I just don't want it to be awkward between us at work."

"Just be cool Ava. Act exactly like you always act around him. You don't want him to think this is a big deal to you otherwise it will be awkward," she says.

"Ok. Normal. Yeah, I can do normal," I say, already knowing I won't be able to act normal. I'm either going to be stand-offish or giggly or something equally bad. "So you don't think I should bring it up?"

"No. God no. How does that show you're cool with what happened? And if he brings it up, just tell him it's done and there's nothing to discuss," Sophie tells me. "You'll be fine, just stop over thinking it. The more you think about it, the more likely you are to be all nervous around him."

She's right about that. I can already feel the nerves in the pit of my stomach. I thought this conversation would make me feel better, but somehow, it's made me more nervous. I think it's because Sophie is just effortlessly cool with stuff like this, but that's because she genuinely isn't embarrassed the next morning after a one night stand. I still kind of am, which makes me overthink it and make a huge deal out of something that Sophie just shrugs off.

"Ok, thanks Soph. I'll let you know how it goes," I say.

"Ok, make sure you do. Good luck," she says and then she ends the call.

Ok, I think to myself. Time to make a move. I'll get to the office hopefully late enough that Christian will already be in, but not late enough to be technically late for work. And once I'm in, I just need to channel my inner Sophie and act like nothing more than a shared meal happened last night with Christian and me.

AVA

I step out of the elevator, taking a deep breath as I go. I greet one of the other secretaries as I move past her desk and then all too soon, I'm heading down the hallway towards my own desk and Christian's office. My legs feel like jelly as I walk along, but I think I hide it well because no one gives me a second glance.

I reach my desk and slip my jacket off and then I sit down and push my purse underneath my desk. I sit still and silent, straining to listen for any sounds coming from Christian's office. I need to know if he's in there or not so I can prepare myself for which way he will come from when I finally do have to face him again.

I can hear the low hum of conversation coming from behind Christian's closed office door. Instead of the rush of relief I was expecting at knowing my plan to have him in before me worked, panic floods through me at the sound of the voices. Have I dropped the ball? Did he have an early morning meeting or something on the one day I decided to show up later than usual?

I fire up my computer, tapping my fingers impatiently as I wait for it to load up. As soon as it does, I open my files and look through Christian's daily planner. There is nothing on there about an early morning meeting or anything and I quickly double check through all of his emails. No. There's nothing in his inbox or anywhere else I would be expected to look that says he had a meeting this morning. It must just be one of the other partners dropped by for some reason. Ok, that's not quite as bad. Arguably I should have been here to field the visit, but it's not like I knew about it in advance and dropped the ball.

Maybe having someone in there with Christian will help me in some ways too. If Christian walks to the door with the person, then we will come face to face in front of someone else and we will have to both act normal. And once that first meeting is done with, it won't be so bad after that.

I try to focus on what I'm supposed to be doing, but it's hard because my mind isn't on it; my mind is well and truly on Christian and what's going to happen once his meeting or whatever this is ends. Is he going to want to talk to me about last night or not? Is he going to pretend like it never happened or is he going to be all awkward and weird about it? Maybe he'll fire me – by being a little late this morning, I guess I've given him a reason to do it if he finds having me around now too awkward. And while technically I'm not late, if he chooses to go down that route, fighting it will just feel way too desperate.

With the possibility, however faint, of losing my job in mind, I force myself to focus on responding to emails and starting my day – I don't want to give Christian any more of a reason to fire me.

I manage to get my head into the right space after a few minutes and by the time Christian's office door opens, I'm lost in my work. I look up from my monitor when the sound of the door opening registers, knowing it will be strange if I don't acknowledge whoever is leaving.

To my delight, the person who steps out of Christian's office is Mr. Kramer. His face breaks into a wide beaming smile when he sees me.

"Mr. Kramer," I say, returning his smile. "How are you? I had no idea you were coming in today. It's so good to see you."

"It was a last minute thing," Mr. Kramer smiles. "And I'm fine thank you. The wife and I are just busy enjoying our retirement. How are you?"

"Good," I smile.

Mr. Kramer nods his head in approval.

"Good to hear," he says. "Now are you going to keep me waiting all day or are you coming around here to give me a hug?"

I laugh and get to my feet, moving around my desk to get to Mr. Kramer. He pulls me into a tight hug. He half releases me and then he beams at me and pulls me in for another hug. He's always been a hugger and I don't mind in the slightest, but the double hug is a new thing. It makes me wonder if he's being entirely honest about his retirement. If he is so enthusiastic to see me, is he really enjoying being away from the office as much as he said he is?

Mr. Kramer releases me the second time and we exchange goodbyes. I'm heading back behind my desk when Mr. Kramer shouts back over his shoulder.

"See you soon Ava," he calls.

"Will do," I reply.

He must be planning on coming in again next week or something, I think to myself. How else would he expect to see me soon? I shake the thought away. It's probably just something he said. I mean I said it back just automatically, so maybe that's all it was with him. I don't suppose it means anything, and even if it does, it isn't my place to question why Mr. Kramer might be coming back in.

Instead, I can't help but wonder why Mr. Kramer left Christian's office on his own. He came out of there in a good mood, so it's not that they have had words or anything. So does that mean that Christian didn't bother walking his father out of his office because he doesn't want to have to face me yet?

Maybe it does mean that, and maybe it doesn't. I don't know, and to be honest, I'm getting a bit sick of stressing out about something I can't control. I'm just going to put my head down and get on with my job and when I see Christian, I'm just going to play it by ear and see how it goes. It's about all I can do short of marching into Christian's office and demanding we talk about last night which I'm certainly not about to do.

My mind made up, I go back to my computer. I find I can focus a little bit better now that I've cleared my mind of thoughts of Christian and I'm soon engrossed in my work once more. I am so engrossed in it in fact, that when Christian finally does emerge from his office, I don't even notice he's stepped out of his office until he speaks to me. His voice breaks the silence of the corridor and I jump slightly, but I recover quickly and look up and smile at him as he says my name.

"Sorry, I was engrossed in this," I smile.

"No need to apologize. Can you come into my office for a moment please? I need to talk to you about something important," Christian says.

I nod my head and stand up. I'm a little bit nervous, but I don't know why. If it wasn't for last night, I wouldn't be. Christian sounds serious but not angry, so I don't think I'm in any trouble. At least I hope I'm not. I guess I'll find out in a second.

As I step around my desk, Christian steps aside and holds the door to his office open for me. I get a whiff of his aftershave and beneath it, the musky scent of his skin and I feel my heart race a little bit faster. I tell myself to stop that right now, but that's much easier to think than it is to do.

I hold my composure as Christian gestures for me to sit down. The fact he's nodding to his seating area rather than the chair opposite his desk makes me think that I'm not about to be fired. Surely he would want me at his desk for something like that, not sitting relaxed in a comfortable armchair.

I sit down and play with the hem of my skirt for a second before I catch myself and force myself to stop. I clasp my hands together so I'm not tempted to fiddle around with them and then I smile at Christian as he sits down opposite me.

"So my dad was here," he says.

"Yes," I say, noting that he looks kind of nervous. I feel better somehow to know that I'm not the only one who is only pretending that everything is cool and normal and not at all awkward. "He spoke to me on the way out."

"What did he say?" Christian asks quickly.

Too quickly. I frown as I reply.

"Nothing really. Just that he was enjoying retirement and then he left," I say.

"Oh good," Christian says, looking relieved. "Sorry, I was just a bit worried he would have hinted at what we were talking about before I had a chance to talk to you about it first."

I wait for Christian to go on. I had no idea what he was talking about so I didn't know what to say to prod him in the right direction and he wasn't exactly rushing to fill me in. Some of my nerves had shifted to slight annoyance now.

"Ok, well I think it's fair to say this is kind of awkward and not at all the conversation I expected us to be having today – or well, anytime really," Christian says. He's doing the nervous babbling I was afraid I would do while I'm sitting here cool, calm and collected. Outwardly at least. "So I'm just going to come right out and say it. My dad saw us kissing last night. On the CCTV, which apparently feeds to his home computer."

I feel the color draining from my face when I think about everything else we did last night. Mr. Kramer saw all of that? My thoughts must be clear to read on my face because Christian hurries on.

"There aren't any cameras in the parking lot. Or at least not ones that go to my dad's feed. It was only the kiss at the front of the building he saw," he says.

That makes me feel slightly better. In fact, it makes me feel a lot better. It's still kind of embarrassing, but it's not like he saw anything really private. And he obviously wasn't pissed off about it. Mr. Kramer isn't the mind game type, so if he was pissed off about me and Christian kissing, he wouldn't have been so nice with me as he left the office.

"Ok," I say. "Well that's awkward, but let's face it – he could have seen a lot worse."

Christian smiles and nods his head.

"Yeah I don't think he would have been quite so chilled out about that," he laughs.

"It's funny," I say. "All this time I've worked here I never knew the CCTV feed went to your dad's home computer."

"I had no idea either. Typical this is the way we find out," Christian says.

He smiles as he says it but he still looks nervous.

"So was there something else or…?" I say after a moment when it becomes clear that he's not in any hurry to speak or dismiss me.

Christian's pause drags on, despite my question and I'm starting to think he's just not going to say anything. Just sitting here is becoming kind of awkward, but getting up and leaving before he's done would be worse. Just when I think I can't handle the silence for a moment longer, Christian finally speaks.

"When I took over this job from my dad, he gave me an ultimatum. He and my mom are apparently concerned that I'm not settled down with a nice girl. For me to keep this job, they want me to find the right girl and be in a serious relationship by the end of one year," Christian says.

Well that explains why Christian was going on a date he didn't seem to want to go on yesterday then. But I have no idea why he's suddenly telling me about this. He's clearly uncomfortable telling me and it's not like I asked, so why is he even bothering.

"Right," I say, not really sure what else to say under the circumstances.

"So after what he saw last night – us kissing - my dad now thinks we're together. And well… I didn't exactly contradict him," Christian says.

"What?" I say. Surely I've misunderstood. But I can't think of anything else Christian could mean except what I think he means. I have to know for sure though, and I cling to a small hope that when I check, Christian will laugh and say that's not what he means at all. "So now your dad thinks we're a couple and you let him believe it to be true?"

Christian nods his head. I don't know what to say. For a moment, I'm just stupefied by the news. I guess that's why Mr. Kramer said he'd see me soon. He thinks I'm his son's girlfriend so he is probably expecting to see me socially. Oh fuck this. I'm not being made out to be some rude, unsocial creature so Christian can go places without me without his parents getting on his case about finding a girlfriend.

"So when are you telling him he's mistaken about us then?" I say.

IONA ROSE

"Well that's the thing," Christian says. "He was so happy and he was saying how happy my mom is going to be too."

He stops talking and I raise an eyebrow.

"So you're not going to tell him you lied? Don't even think about telling him I dumped you and make me out to be the bad guy here Christian," I say.

"No, no, I wouldn't do anything like that," Christian says quickly. "But I don't want to disappoint them. And I really don't want to lose my job here. So I have a proposition for you. Go along with it. Pretend to be my girlfriend. Do that for one year and I will pay you one hundred thousand dollars."

AVA

I throw my head back and laugh when Christian suggests I pretend to be his girlfriend for a year in exchange for money. I honestly can't help myself. I mean it's just the most ridiculous thing I've ever heard. Christian frowns at me as I laugh and that just makes me laugh harder, like how does he not see that this is fucking ridiculous. Eventually my laughter starts to die down and I dab at my now wet eyes.

"Are you done?" Christian says, one eyebrow raised.

I nod my head although I'm not sure I'm not going to burst into giggles again at any moment.

"So let me get this straight. You would rather spend a hundred thousand dollars and live a full year of your life in a lie rather than just tell your dad that we kissed and that was it, we're not an item?" I say.

"Yes," Christian says. "And not just because I don't want to upset him and mom. It's a perfect solution. They're happy that I'm happy and I will be happy when I'm not constantly trying to find my soulmate or whatever. Everyone wins Ava."

"Right. And what exactly do I get out of this?" I say. "What's my prize?"

"A hundred thousand dollars," Christian reminds me.

I have to admit it's tempting. A hundred thousand dollars is a lot of money. Hell it's more than I'll make in three years here as my normal salary. There's so much I could do with the money. I could redecorate my whole apartment, upgrade my car, put some aside for rainy days, go on a vacation or two. I could really use that money.

But do I really want to sell myself like that? Do I want to become a glorified hooker for a year? Ok, maybe not a hooker. I'm sure Christian doesn't expect me to sleep with him, but I would certainly be a glorified escort. And it would mean lying to Mr. Kramer, the one person who has given me so much at this firm.

And then of course there's the stigma attached to being one of those women who sleeps with her boss. Do I want that hanging over my head here? Do I want the other girls whispering and gossiping about me? Saying I only got to where I am now because I'm sleeping with Christian. Having said that, I was already in this role long before Christian started here, so it's not like I can be accused of sleeping with the boss to get ahead.

There would still be talk, but the amount of money I've been offered kind of makes a bit of harmless gossip seem like less of an issue. And at the end of the year, we could come up with some story about wanting different things or something so we can break up with both of our reputations still intact.

I realize with a start that for a second there, I was actually seriously considering this. But I can't actually go through with it. I can't live a lie for a full year. And the fact that this is the most ridiculous thing I've ever heard hasn't changed either.

"I'm sorry Christian, I can't do that. I'm afraid you'll have to tell your parents the truth," I say.

I stand up and head for the door.

"Ava, wait," Christian says. "We need to talk. You can't just walk away like this."

I glance back at him.

"Is the talk about work or about this ridiculous idea of yours?" I ask.

Christian won't meet my eye and the way he pauses without answering tells me everything I need to know about what he wanted to talk to me about. I shake my head.

"There's nothing left to say about that. Let's just pretend this conversation didn't happen," I say.

I put my hand on the door handle, but before I can open it, Christian has followed me and closed the gap between us. He puts his hand on the door, preventing me from opening it. He is so close that I can smell the delicious scent of him once again and once more, the scent of him affects me in ways I would rather it didn't. My heart races, my pussy gets wet and I feel my cheeks flushing slightly. I don't know how he affects me so easily. Maybe it's because the memory of last night is still so fresh in my mind.

God I wish he would lean down and kiss me. Slam me up against the door and fuck the life out of me. But then again, if he kissed me now, I know he would be able to get me to agree to anything, and with such a crazy plan on the table, that's not a good position to be in. It doesn't matter anyway though, because of course he doesn't kiss me and I push aside the thoughts of the orgasms he gives me ripping through my body. With an effort, I recover my senses and I glare at him.

"Take your hand off the door," I say.

My voice has a slight quiver to it, the lust I feel is not so easy to swallow away completely, but if Christian notices it, he doesn't comment on it.

"The end of the day," Christian says, ignoring me.

His statement confuses me enough that for the moment, I'm more focused on that than the fact he is still essentially holding me against my will in his office.

"What about it?" I say.

He better not think for even a second that I'm going to stand for being fired for this. If he means I have until the end of the day to get everything sorted and clear my desk out, then he is in for a big surprise because I'm not going anywhere. And if he tries it, I won't be keeping quiet. I will be quite happy to tell everyone exactly why he is firing me, and because I haven't done anything wrong work wise, it will be hard for Christian to refute my claims because there's no other reason for him to randomly decide to fire me.

"Don't give me a definite no yet. Just take until the end of the day to think about it," he says.

Ok, that's not as bad as I thought it was going to be, but waiting until the end of the day isn't going to change anything and I don't want to string him along. Still though, at least he's not trying to fire me. I need to stop jumping to conclusions. At least I didn't start ranting and raving though.

"I don't need to take until the end of the day. I've already thought about it and the answer is no," I say firmly.

Obviously I don't say it firmly enough because Christian is still going on.

"You haven't thought about it properly. You haven't had time to consider it fully and obviously with me sitting there waiting for an answer, the pressure was on and that wouldn't have helped you look at all of the angles," he says. "Look, I'm not saying you will change your mind, and if you don't, then I'll talk to my dad, tell him the truth, and there will be no hard feelings. But please don't just dismiss the idea without giving it a real chance. That's all I'm asking. Come on, am I really that hideous that the thought of being my pretend girl-friend for like eight hours freaks you out this much?"

I know he's joking about being hideous but I still shake my head.

"It's not that," I say.

"I know," he says. "So is that a yes then? To the end of the day?"

I think for a moment.

"I…" I start.

"Just until the end of the day. Please," Christian says, cutting me off before I can finish my sentence.

"I was going to say I can give you until the end of the day," I smile.

Christian beams at me and I feel like he's confident that I will say yes given the extra time. I don't think I will change my mind. It's just easier to give him the extra few hours if that's what it takes to convince him I'm serious about my no thank you. I don't want to give him any room to say I implied I was going to do it or anything though.

"But please don't get your hopes up. I promise I will think about it, but I really don't see me changing my mind about things," I say, trying to prepare him for another no later on today.

"That's all I ask, and then if you do still say no, at least I know you've thought about it properly and not just had a knee jerk reaction," he says.

I nod my head and wait for him to move his hand off the door. I look up at him when he doesn't and our eyes meet. I'm mesmerized by him as he holds me in his gaze. He starts to lean forward and I move to meet him, needing to feel his lips on mine. He is less than an inch from kissing me when a loud knock on the door startles us. We jump apart and Christian calls out a come in.

We look at each other in the split second before the door opens and as it opens, we are both laughing. I quickly excuse myself as Mr. Foley comes into the office and I go back to my desk. If I thought concentrating on my work had been hard before, it was next to impossible now with Christian's offer hanging over my head. Not to mention our almost kiss and the fact we would have been caught by Mr. Foley if we had kissed.

Once Mr. Foley has left Christian's office and I'm not so worried about being seen doing nothing by a managing partner – I'm not counting Christian at this moment as he's the one who has me so distracted I can't focus on my work and he must know this – I stop even trying to focus on work for a moment. Instead, I pick up my note book and flick to a clean sheet of paper. I grab a pen and begin listing the pros and cons of the arrangement.

I start with the cons: Number one, I'll be living a lie. Number two, I'll be the subject of office gossip – not the worst thing that could happen but something I'd rather avoid if possible. Number three, I'll be deceiving Mr. Kramer.

I look at the list for a moment and then with a shrug I start with the pros: Number one, the money. Number two, … and that's as far as I get on the pros list.

It's fair to say it's not exactly a long list of pros, but the money is a huge pro. Maybe it could count as multiple points. But even then, does it outweigh the cons? That's the bit I still can't decide.

I sit staring at the lists, tapping my pen against my front tooth. Almost unbidden, my hand drifts down to the paper and before I know it, I am writing in the pros column, expanding on the empty point number two. The pen scratches over the paper and makes a C and then an H shape and then I slam the pen down. What the hell?

I shake my head. I don't know what my subconscious was playing at there but it wasn't going to write Christian. No way. Just no. I have to say no to this. I'm going crazy. But first, I have to get out of here, out of this office. I need some fresh air.

I grab my purse and start along the corridor. I'm a quarter of the way along when I tell myself this is ridiculous and I just need to relax. I was just doodling, nothing more nothing less, and it makes sense that Christian's name might make an appearance because he was on my mind as I pondered my decision about him. Surely someone who had just given someone an offer like the one he had just given me would be playing on anyone's subconscious mind.

AVA

I check my watch. It's just now four pm. Now technically, most days I will be here until at least seven or eight o'clock, but the working day officially ends at five, and I have a feeling that Christian is going to come looking for my answer at five – I can't see him wanting to wait any longer than that even though waiting at all was his idea not mine. The trouble is, I'm no closer to making the decision than I was when I sat down and made my pros and cons lists. I should have just stuck to the no I gave Christian in his office, but I did promise him that I would think about it and so I have. A fat lot of good that has done me though. Whichever way I find myself leaning, I berate myself and tell myself not to rush into anything, and then I end up leaning the other way. Back and forth, back and forth, a lone ship on a rough sea. Honestly, I'm starting to feel sea sick thinking about this, like I really am being thrown first one way and then the other.

When I lean towards yes, I remind myself that the whole thing is a ridiculous scenario and I couldn't possibly give

Christian a year of my life. And then I lean towards no and I ask myself if Christian is really so bad that I can't spend the odd date night with him here and there in exchange for more money than I could ever imagine having in one go.

I know what I need to do. I need to talk through the decision with someone. But who? Naturally my mind goes to Sophie as my best friend, but will she have any more clue about whether or not this is a good idea than I have? It's not like it's ever happened to her or anyone else we know. But that's the thing. It hasn't happened to anyone I know, so Sophie is as good as anyone else for advice on this.

I grab my cell phone and get up from my desk. I think about grabbing my pros and cons list from my drawer, but the truth is I don't need it; I know it word for word. I make my way to the kitchen at the far end of the floor, the one that's usually deserted at this time of the day. I'm not disappointed. I slip in, grab myself a bottle of water, and sit down at the table.

I crack open the bottle and sip the water and then I call Sophie.

"Don't tell me. You acted like a school girl and he laughed at you and broke your heart into a thousand pieces so you quit on the spot," Sophie says as she takes my call.

"Not exactly," I laugh.

"But something has happened, hasn't it?" she asks.

"Yeah. That's an understatement. You're not going to believe this but Christian has basically asked me to pretend to be his girlfriend for a year," I say. "And in exchange, I get a hundred thousand dollars."

"Holy fucking shit Ava, you are going to be loaded. How is it that you always land on your feet with money? So, when are we going shopping then?" Sophie says.

Her excitement is contagious and I find myself laughing, but then I remember my dilemma and I compose myself.

"So I assume that you think I should do it?" I say.

"Well duh," Sophie says. "Obviously. Wait, are you telling me that you've said no to this? Oh God Ava, tell me that you haven't already said no to this."

"I did originally say no," I admit. "But then Christian asked me to take until the end of the day to think about it and I said I would."

"So here's how I see it. You claim not to like him, yet you've slept with him twice now, so I'm going to assume you can tolerate him to enough of an extent to look pretty on his arm when he needs you to. And in exchange for that, you get a life changing amount of money," Sophie says. She makes it sound so simple, like accepting the offer is a no brainer. "Oh, but wait. This all sounds too good to be true. What's the catch?"

"What do you mean?" I ask. "There is no catch."

"So Christian just randomly decided he wants a fake girl-friend?" Sophie says.

"Oh no. His parents want him to settle down, and then his dad saw us kissing last night, and things kind of went from there," I say.

"You know what Ava? You only live once. Do it. And if you decide it's too awkward to stay working with him once the year is up, it's not like you won't have enough money to take your time and find another place to work is it?" Sophie says.

I look up as the kitchen door opens and three associates come in. They smile at me and I smile back at them.

"You're not alone anymore, are you?" Sophie says.

"No," I reply, glad she's heard the chatter as the associates came in making her less likely to blurt something out loudly enough for them to hear her.

"Right, then you should probably go. But I say go for it. Oh, and one more thing," she says.

"Yeah?" I reply.

"How desperate did he seem for you to do this? Like on a scale of one to ten," she asks.

"I don't know. Pretty desperate. Like a nine or a ten," I say.

"Well in that case, if you do decide to do it, play hard to get for a bit. I reckon you can get at least twice that amount of money out of him," she says.

"That's a bit steep," I say.

Sophie laughs.

"Of course it isn't. Come on girl, I know you are not that naïve. Do you really think Christian opened with the maximum amount he was willing to pay? He's a lawyer for fuck sake. That's just a starting point for the negotiation," she says. "Now don't fuck this up Ava. I'm already planning what I'm buying when you take me shopping."

The call ends in my ear and I pull my cell phone away. I sit for another minute, listening to the easy chatter of the associates, and then I get up and head back to my desk. I'm feeling more confident now that I've talked to Sophie and she has made me see that once again, I'm over-thinking things.

By the time I reach my desk, I've let go of all the worry and the uncertainty, and I'm leaning much more to the side of yes. But Sophie had a point though. One hundred thousand dollars is a lot of money for me, but it's nothing for Christian. It's probably his monthly bonus for fuck sake. And if he wants me to go along with his plan, then his wallet will have to show me just how serious he is about it.

CHRISTIAN

I 've been watching the clock all day, waiting for it to get to five o'clock. It feels like it's taken about eight days rather than about eight hours. I know why today has dragged and it's nothing to do with work. It's because Ava said that she would give me until the end of the day to make her decision and give me a final answer.

We all know that around here, the end of the working day is often at eleven o'clock at night, but I have a feeling that Ava will come to me at five o'clock – the time most civilized jobs call the end of the business day. And when she does, I have a feeling that she's going to say no to my proposal. But I can't let that happen. I just can't go to my dad and tell him that I lied to him about Ava and me being a thing. And I definitely can't just sit back and watch this company be taken away from me and handed over to Lewis goddamned Foley. I can't do it. I won't do it. Not while I still have a chance to get myself out of this potential mess.

I look at the clock again. It's four thirty-two now, two minutes later than the last time I checked the clock. And I know fine well what Ava is like - she's stubborn for starters, fiercely independent for seconds – and if I let her come in here and give me a no at five o'clock, then I don't think I will ever get her to change her mind. But there's a chance she might still say yes if I can get to her before she says a definite no, if I can make her see the advantages of saying yes to this. Then hopefully she'll be just as headstrong and stubborn on her yes decision and she'll be as committed as I am to making this thing work.

I stand up quickly before I can change my mind about this crazy plan that's starting to form in my head. I put my jacket on and walk briskly out of my office. Ava looks up at me as I march towards her. She frowns in confusion as I reach out, take her hand and pull her to her feet. I don't speak, don't explain, I just pull on her hand so she's walking along the corridor with me. We are almost at the elevators when Ava regains her senses.

"What the hell are you doing?" she demands. I don't reply, I just keep looking straight ahead, keep walking. "Hey. Christian. What the hell?"

I still don't answer her and she tries to pull her hand out of mine. I grip her hand a little bit tighter – not enough to hurt her, just enough to let her know I'm not giving up without a fight - and she sighs.

"Ok. Fine. I'll come with you if it's so important. I just want to know where we are going," she says. "And why you abducted me rather than just telling me what was going on in the first place?"

I still don't answer her. We reach the elevators and stand waiting for one. I allow Ava to free her hand from mine as it would look awfully weird to any of the other partners if they step out of the elevator to me and Ava standing holding hands, but I still don't tell her anything. I glance at her out of the corner of my eye. She looks like she's a rolling mixture of silently fuming and confused as hell. I bite the inside of my lip to stop myself from smiling. At least now I know how to throw her off kilter. It's good to know I can throw her off balance like she can do to me so easily.

The elevator arrives and we step inside. I hit the button for the lobby. I look at Ava. She opens her mouth, presumably to ask me once more what's going on, but she sees my amused look and shuts her mouth again. I wonder what would happen if I kissed her. Would she kiss me back? I honestly think she would, but I can't do it. I can't even think about doing it. Not if I want her to play her part in our fake relationship. We can't have blurred lines with something like that. Someone will end up getting hurt. And that someone is likely to be me.

The elevator reaches the lobby and I step out. I take a few steps and then I realize that Ava isn't with me anymore. I glance back to see what's keeping her. She's still in the elevator. She smiles at me and leans towards the control panel. Oh she wants to play. Ok, I'll play. I shrug my shoulders and turn away from her, walking across the lobby again.

"Goddamn you Christian," I hear Ava say under breath as she gets out of the elevator despite herself.

I smile to myself, pleased that my nonchalance has worked and got Ava's curiosity up enough that she couldn't help but follow me. I step out of the lobby and outside into the cool, late afternoon air. I move to the side of the road and I look both ways. The street is quiet and I go to cross the road, but I feel a hand grab my wrist and I pause. I know it's Ava holding my wrist. I can tell by the tingles her touch sends up my arm.

"I'm not going any further with you until you tell me exactly what is going on here," she says.

"I'm grabbing a burger from the diner across the street. I thought you might like one," I say.

She relaxes her grip and shakes her head.

"And you couldn't just tell me that?" she says.

"Oh no I could have. I just thought this way would be more fun," I say with a grin.

Ava shakes her head again, but she's smiling this time and then she shrugs her shoulders.

"Ok, come on then," she says. She steps onto the road and then smiles over her shoulder at me as she walks. "But something that's normal in size this time."

I smile and nod. We go into the diner and take a booth and we order cheeseburgers and sodas. Once our order is taken, Ava turns her attention back to me.

"So what's really going on here?" she asks.

"I really wanted a burger," I smile. Ava rolls her eyes and I laugh softly. "Ok, ok. I guess I wanted to talk to you away from the office about the offer I made you this morning."

I watch her to gauge her reaction, but she gives very little away, she just nods her head once.

"I figured as much," she says. "So talk."

Before I can start, our waitress shows up with our drinks and our burgers. We thank her and then I pick up my burger and take a big bite. Ava nibbles on hers too and we eat in silence for a moment. I'm about halfway through my burger when I start to talk.

"So I'm assuming you still have some doubts about saying yes to my offer," I say.

Ava nods her head but she doesn't speak and so I go on.

"And do you care to share those doubts?" I say gently.

"I…" Ava starts and then she sighs and shakes her head and starts over again. "I mean the whole thing is just crazy."

"Is it?" I say.

"Yes," she says without any hesitation. "I mean come on. You're going to pay me to pretend to be your girlfriend. You could find an actual girlfriend and spoil her rotten for a year and spend less money than what you've offered me."

"I'm aware of that, but with a real girlfriend comes problems. I don't want to spend the next year arguing with someone every time I work late, or trying to keep her sweet when I forget her birthday or any of that crap. And I certainly don't want her getting sick of me and ending things before I get the business signed over to me," I say. "So yeah, I'm aware of what you're saying, but I would rather pay the money and get what I need without all of the messy parts."

Ava takes a bite of her burger and chews it slowly, her brow furrowed as she thinks for a moment before responding to me. I hope the fact she is considering my words rather than giving me an outright, immediate no is a good thing. I think it is. I hope it is.

"Ok, that makes sense I suppose," she concedes.

"So that's a yes then?" I say with a smile, not really believing it's going to be this easy but still relieved that it's still not a no at this point.

"I didn't say that," Ava replies quickly.

"No I know you didn't, but you said it makes sense. Why wouldn't you do something if doing it makes sense?" I say.

"Things like this can get complicated Christian and I don't want that. There would have to be rules," Ava says.

I know this is still far from a done deal, but I feel the atmosphere change in the room and now the diner is filled with a kind of nervous anticipation. I actually think Ava might end up saying yes to this if I can make her see that actually, it doesn't need to be complicated at all. My heart races in my chest as I tell myself not to fuck this up.

"What sort of rules?" I ask.

If I let her take the lead and find out what she's most afraid of throughout this arrangement, then I can find a way to reassure her. She thinks for a moment and then she shrugs her shoulders and turns her attention back to the last of her burger.

"No, come on," I say. "You must have some idea of the kind of rules you would want in place to make you feel comfortable. You wouldn't have brought it up if you didn't."

"Fine. At the end of the year, we break up amicably and we remain friends," Ava says. "I don't want to be made out to be the bad guy that broke your heart and equally I don't want to be the sad little victim who got dumped."

"Ok," I agree. "That's fine."

"And there can be no cheating," Ava says. "If you want me to give up a year of my life to act like your girlfriend, then you have to be willing to do the same for me. I won't be taken for a fool, not even a pretend one. I won't have my friends and family feeling pity for me because they think my boyfriend is cheating on me and I just put up with it."

"Ok," I say again. "And that one would have to work both ways for the same reason."

Ava nods her head curtly. Am I starting to get her closer to giving me a yes? I think I might be but I don't want to get my hopes up yet. Oh who am I kidding? My hopes are already well and truly up.

"One more thing," Ava says. She pauses and I wait, hardly daring to breathe. This is it. If this rule is something else like the others that I can happily live with like the other two were then I reckon we're on. "I want one hundred and fifty thousand dollars for the year, not one hundred thousand dollars."

"Done," I say without hesitation.

Ava's jaw drops open and then she smiles a little bit shyly. She looks so vulnerable, so cute, I want to wrap her in my arms and kiss her. I resist the urge of course and instead, I hold my hand out to her.

"Ava Long, will you be my fake girlfriend?" I say with a smile.

Ava nods and smiles back at me, shaking my outstretched hand.

"I will," she says "Until next year do us part."

We both laugh at Ava's twisted wedding vow and then we fall into a companionable silence. Ava breaks the silence after a few minutes.

"So what happens now?" she asks.

"I guess the first thing is getting you a decent dress for my dad's charity gala," I reply.

"See I want to be offended that you don't think I'd have something suitable already but well, you're right so I can't be upset really can I?" Ava grins.

I laugh and shake my head.

"Nope," I say. "Besides, let's be honest Ava, you could wear sweats and a hoodie and still be the hottest person in the room. The dress is just a bonus for you."

Ava laughs and shakes her head but she's blushing and I can tell she's pleased with my compliment. And it's true. She could turn up in anything and still be the hottest person in any room.

"When's the gala?" Ava asks.

"Tomorrow night," I reply.

"Tomorrow night? But that's like... tomorrow," Ava blurts out.

"Umm no shit," I grin.

Ava laughs but then she turns serious again.

"I mean that's not much time to get a dress sorted and have my hair and nails and everything done," she says.

"Relax," I say. "We'll get your dress ordered tonight and there's nothing wrong with your hair and nails as they are."

Ava raises an eyebrow and I laugh and hold my hands up in defeat.

"Ok, I admit I have no idea about stuff like that. But I mean tomorrow is Saturday. You'll have all day to get everything done I tell her. "I realize it's short notice, but you'll be able to get everything done I'm sure. And you'll have an expenses card naturally so you don't have to worry about where you go being too expensive or anything like that."

"Ok, I can make it work," Ava smiles. "I wouldn't exactly be the right person for the job if I fell at the first hurdle would I."

"That's the spirit," I grin. "Now let's go and get you a dress."

I wave to the waitress and signal for the check.

"I've left all of my stuff at the office," Ava says. "And I still have work to do."

"Work that can wait or not?" I ask.

"It can wait," she says. "But I really do need my stuff. My cell phone, my apartment keys, my car keys. They're all in there."

"That's ok, you can collect them before we leave," I say as I pay the check and leave a generous tip.

We stand up and leave the diner and head back towards the office. When we get there, Ava goes inside and I go to the parking lot to wait for her. I can't quite believe she said yes to this. I have to wonder what she would have said if I had just asked her to be my girlfriend. Would she have said yes to that? I'd like to hope that she would have, but who knows? I didn't dare risk it because if I did ask her that and she said no, then I knew there was no chance of her agreeing to be my fake girlfriend. And besides, this way is just less complicated. There's a whole lot riding on this and I don't want to get it wrong and hurt Ava or lose my half of the firm.

And maybe this is the best way to do it. Think of it as like a year's trial run of a relationship. And at the end of the year, if I think there's even a chance Ava might want to stick around as my real girlfriend, then I can ask her then without all of the added pressure.

I jump slightly when there's a tap at my car window but then I see its Ava and I smile and roll the window down.

"Get in then," I say.

"I'll follow you in my car," she says. "And then you don't have to bring me back here after we've looked at the dresses."

"Ok, good idea," I agree.

I wait, watching as Ava cuts across the parking lot. She hits her unlock button on her fob and a car's lights flash. She gets in and I start my engine and pull out of the space. Ava does the same and I pull out onto the main street with her behind me. She's still on my tail when we reach my building. We head inside and Ava sits on the couch. I hand her my laptop.

"Would you like a drink or anything?" I ask.

"No thank you," she says. She nods at the laptop. "Where do I start?"

I laugh softly.

"Believe it or not Ava, women's dresses and where to buy them from isn't really my specialist subject," I tell her.

"And believe it or not, knowing where to shop for an event I don't have any idea of the dress code for isn't exactly my specialist subject either," Ava laughs.

"Ok, fair point," I say.

I sit down beside her and gently take the laptop from her. I open up my Instagram account and scroll through the pictures until I find some from my father's last charity gala. I pass the laptop back to Ava.

"So this is the kind of thing people wear to these things," I say.

She studies the photos and nods.

"Right. Full on formal evening gowns," she says.

She's quiet for a moment, studying the photos and then she opens up another tab and gets to work searching for a dress.

"Do you like this one?" she asks after a moment, pointing to a pretty, light green dress. I nod my head but before I can speak, she's already shaking hers. "No, scrap that. It would look nice on someone else, but with my hair, I'd be worried I looked like Ariel."

"Who the hell is Ariel?" I ask.

"The Little Mermaid," Ava giggles.

I shake my head and laugh with her.

"Right. And you expected me just to know that did you?" I say.

She goes back to the website and keeps flicking through more and more dresses, rejecting them for a bunch of reasons that make no sense to me. I haven't seen a single dress she wouldn't look gorgeous in yet.

Dress shopping isn't exactly on the top of my fun things to do list at the best of times and I find myself distracted from it pretty quickly. And how could I not be distracted, even if the activity was something I actually liked doing, when so close to me that we're almost touching. At first, I was trying to imagine how she would look in the dresses she kept showing me, but in all honesty, that soon went out of the window and I found myself instead remembering how she looks without anything on.

I find myself aching for her and it's all I can do not to reach out and touch her. I want to so badly but I'm afraid to do it in case she doesn't want me to. It would be too embarrassing if she rejects me and then I have to go and play the role of her boyfriend tomorrow. And worse, what if she doesn't want to but she goes along with it thinking it's a part of the deal?

I stand up abruptly before I can let myself pull Ava towards me and kiss her. She looks up and for a moment, I see a flicker of disappointment on her face. Ok then so maybe she wouldn't be so quick to reject my advances after all and if she didn't, then judging by her expression now, it wouldn't be because she felt obligated to provide some added bonuses to our deal.

"I'm just going to grab you one of my cards while I remember," I say.

I really do need to sort out a card for Ava and the excuse reminds me to go and do it. I go through to my home office and dig through my top drawer until I find my spare cards. I choose one with a good spending limit on it and write down the pin number for Ava. I go back through to the living room. Ava looks up as I enter, a big smile on her face.

"What?" I say, automatically returning her smile, even though I have no idea why she's suddenly so happy.

"I've found the one," she says. "The perfect dress."

I go back to the couch and take my seat beside Ava again. She turns the laptop towards me slightly so that I can see the screen and then she points to one of the dresses. It's long and satiny, midnight blue in colour. The neckline plunges down but tastefully so. The dress is long, but I can't help but notice the thigh high split on it. This girl is going to be the death of me. I can barely keep my hands off her in her pencil skirt and shirt from work. How the hell am I supposed to resist her when I see her in that?

"Don't you like it?" she asks, her face crumpling and I realize I've been too quiet for too long.

"I love it," I say quickly. "Really. I was just picturing you in it."

"And…" she prompts.

The air is suddenly charged and I can almost smell the sex in the air as I breathe in a shaky breath.

"And it looks amazing on you," I say. I swallow hard. "But you look even better with it off."

Ava searches my face for a moment, her lips slightly parted, her cheeks flushed. I watch her, my breath catching in my throat. I'm just about to lean in when Ava laughs softly.

"Charmer," she says.

It shatters the sexual tension but it also makes me laugh and I love how Ava can always seem to surprise me. I hold my hands up in mock surrender.

"It's all true," I laugh. I hand her the card. "Here you go. You can put your new dress on there."

"Thanks," she says.

She takes the card and turns her attention back to the laptop. I watch her as she adds the dress to her basket and goes through to the checkout screen. She enters the card details and her address details. She selects next day delivery and then she's done. She smiles at me as the confirmation message pops up on the screen.

"Well, it looks like Cinderella will be going to the ball after all," she says. She nods to the laptop. "Do you mind if I check my emails real quick? I always worry anything I order isn't going to come until I've seen the confirmation email."

"No, I don't mind at all," I say.

She shuffles forward slightly and her fingers dance over the keys as she types. I can't stop myself from watching her and my eyes keep straying to the bare skin above her collar. Her hand comes up and rubs her neck and it's like we're acting as one, like me thinking of her neck made her feel it. I don't know if it's truly a sign or not, but I take it as one and I lean closer to Ava.

I put my hand on her shoulder and gently kiss her neck. I hear the clicking of the keyboard stop. I kiss down Ava's neck and push the collar of her blouse down so I can reach the untouched skin beneath it.

Abruptly, Ava jumps up from the couch and puts the laptop on the coffee table. I jump up too. I can't believe I've managed to piss her off already. I open my mouth to apologize to her and promise her that I won't let that happen again, but before I can speak, Ava grins at me. It's a wicked looking grin that sends a rush of lust through me.

Ava reaches out and grabs my tie. She turns away from me, holding it above her shoulder and she begins to walk, leading me towards my bedroom and now I'm so glad I gave in and kissed her neck. And I'm so glad she's my fake girlfriend.

As we reach my bedroom door, Ava glances back at me and grins.

"You know, I could get used to this arrangement," she says and then she leads me into my bedroom and I kick the door shut behind us.

AVA

I knew from the moment I agreed to this whole deal that we would end up in Christian's bed at some point this evening. For a moment though, I began to think I'd misread the signs. We had a heated moment, a moment where I really thought Christian would kiss me but he didn't; he seemed to get cold feet at the last minute and pulled back from me. It got me thinking that maybe nothing would happen after all. But then he kissed my neck and I knew I had been right all along. He had just been waiting for the right moment.

After I led Christian to his bedroom, it didn't take long for our clothes to come off. It was like a whirlwind of fabric as we ripped at each other's clothes and at our own clothes. Within seconds of the bedroom door closing behind us, we are both naked and Christian has laid me on his bed.

He pulls at my ankles and I slide along the sheet until I am laying on my back with my legs hanging over the edge of the bed from the knees. Christian kneels between my open legs. He runs his hands over my thighs, sending goosebumps chasing each other lazily over my skin. He moves closer to my center and as he does, his fingers caress more sensitive skin. Just when I think I can't take his tickling, teasing touch anymore, he leans his head down and pushes my knees further apart.

When I am spread wide open for him, he leans even closer to me and I feel the rough warmth of his tongue running over my exposed clit. I gasp in a breath, surprised at how sensitive I am to Christian's touch. My clit is swollen, filled with need and Christian knows exactly how to satisfy that need. He rubs his tongue back and forth over my clit and then side to side, sending shocks of pleasure through my body.

He licks me for a while longer and then he pushes two fingers inside of me as he works my clit. He moves his fingers in time with his tongue and then he reaches up with his other hand and gently works my nipple between his thumb and his fore finger.

I can hardly breathe as pleasure assaults me from all directions. I gasp and pant, my hips writhing, pressing myself tighter against Christian's tongue, needing the release now. He seems to sense the urgent need in me and he ups the pace of his licking. His fingers slip in and out of me faster too. He presses his tongue down on my clit at the same time as his fingers find my G spot and I moan as my orgasm floods through me.

I feel Christian's fingers slip out of me and his hand leaves my breast. He lifts his face up from between my legs and smiles at me. I can see my juices shining on his lips and when he climbs on top of me and kisses me, I can taste myself on his tongue.

He pushes his cock inside of me as he kisses me and I gasp in a breath as he fills me. He begins to thrust and I thrust with him, loving the feeling of him moving inside of me. His thrusts soon become faster and I know he's close to orgasming, but I'm not ready for this to end.

I buck my hips, throwing Christian to the side. I go with him and roll him onto his back. He stays inside of me as we roll and I end up straddling him just as I planned to. I start to raise myself and then lower myself, impaling myself on Christian's cock. I move up and down slowly, savoring the moment, the movement. Christian moans in frustration as I drag out the moment, making him wait for his release.

He opens his eyes and peers up at me and I smile at him. He shakes his head, but he smiles anyway. I keep moving, long slow movements that bring Christian right to the edge of my pussy and then push him all of the way back in. He puts his hands on my hips trying to move me faster, but for now, I resist his touch and keep moving at my own pace.

I lean forward and gently rub my nipples over Christian's chest, a feather light touch that makes him moan. I run my lips over his and then I sit back up. I start to move faster now, letting Christian slide closer and closer to his climax. I can tell by the way his breathing changes that he's right on the verge of orgasming and I start to slow my pace again, but this time, Christian isn't letting me call the shots and he grabs my hips and rolls me until he's back on top of me. He thrusts into me quickly until his climax comes over him. His face twists as ecstasy floods his body. His muscles tighten, his body rigid. He moans my name and then his body relaxes and he slips out of me and rolls to the side and flops down onto the bed beside me.

We lay side by side catching our breaths for a moment. I turn my head when I hear Christian shifting slightly. He's rolled onto his side facing me and his head is propped up on his hand. He smiles down at me and I smile up at him. He leans down and kisses my forehead and then he comes back up looking serious now.

"We shouldn't have done that," he says.

"I know. It was truly awful," I agree.

Christian frowns and I can't keep my laughter in any longer.

"I'm joking," I say. I turn serious. "But yeah, you're probably right that we shouldn't have done it."

"I think so," Christian says. "We can't let ourselves blur the lines between a business arrangement such as what we have and an actual relationship. Because as soon as feelings start getting involved, then someone is bound to end up getting hurt."

"Are you seriously suggesting I can't possibly have sex with you without falling in love with you?" I say with a raised eyebrow.

"No, quite the opposite," Christian replies. "I want to make sure I don't get hurt."

I don't think for a second that Christian seriously thinks he will fall for me and get his heart broken, but I kind of like the way he's pretending he thinks that might be the case so I can save face. He clearly thinks I will end up falling for him and getting hurt. And maybe he's right. It's going to be hard to be around someone who I find so attractive and act the part as their girlfriend and not get at least a little bit attached to him. Add sex into the mix and really, what's the difference between what we're doing and what real couples are doing?

"Seriously Ava, I don't want this to get awkward. Can we just agree that we shouldn't have sex again, or at least that we shouldn't have sex again for the next year while we have a business arrangement in place?" Christian says.

I know he's right. That's what my head says we should. My heart isn't sure. And my pussy screams at me not to make such a stupid deal; of course we're going to end up having sex again. It's almost inevitable. Still though, Christian is probably right. We should at least try to keep our relationship strictly platonic.

"Ok," I agree.

"You look kind of upset about it. Are you ok?" he says.

I can see the mischievous glint in his eye and I know he's joking. He doesn't really think I'm that upset about this.

"I'll live," I tell him with a grin. "I mean it'll be hard to resist you, but if that's what I have to do then I'll do it."

"You know sarcasm can hurt a person's feelings," Christian laughs.

"Who said I was being sarcastic," I say with a grin.

Christian shakes his head and laughs.

"Ok, let's see how clever you are when you have to try and resist my touch," he says.

He runs his fingers up my stomach sending a delicious shiver through my body. I try my best to hide the effect he has on me and I think I must have succeeded because Christian doesn't stop even though technically, he's made his point. I genuinely try to resist his touch, but I feel my body responding to him, and almost of its own accord, my back arches, pushing me tighter against Christian's hand.

I look up at him, expecting to see a smug smile and then for him to laugh and say I told you so. Instead, he leans down to me and before I know it, our lips are locked on each other's once more. Christian moves his hand back down over my stomach and pushes his fingers between my lips, rubbing my sensitive, swollen clit. I moan into his mouth, a sound that is part pain, part longing and all pleasure.

He keeps rubbing me until I'm about to climax, my whole body tingling and longing for release and then he pulls his hand away. Before I can react, Christian is on top of me and he's inside of me once more, pumping his hips, filling my pussy and pushing me over the edge. I cry out his name as my orgasm consumes me. I feel all of my muscles turning rigid, my back arching and my pussy clenching. I feel a rush of warm liquid as I reach the peak of my pleasure. I close my eyes, thrusting in time with Christian as I coast down from my orgasm.

Christian orgasms not long behind me and then we lay side by side again. This time, I'm the one to turn towards him once I've gotten my breath back. He turns his head as I turn towards him and as we meet each other's eye, we both start laughing.

"I mean I knew when we said no more sex that it was going to happen again, but I thought we would have lasted a bit longer than that," I say.

"Yeah that has to be the record for the worst attempt at sticking to something," Christian agrees.

As our laughter fades and I find myself staying in place, watching Christian, smiling to myself at our closeness, I know he's right. We have to make this no sex thing work or one of us, most likely me, is going to get hurt.

"So the rules count from now then?" I say.

"Yeah," Christian says. "I guess they do."

I don't know if I'm just hearing disappointment in his voice because I kind of want to, but I swear Christian doesn't sound overly happy about the idea of us sticking to the rules. Maybe we should just abandon them altogether. No I tell myself. This is a business arrangement and I need to start treating it like one.

I get up off the bed and get dressed. I know Christian is watching me, but I resist the urge to put on a show for him. We have to be able to get through one night without breaking the rules for goodness sake. Christian seems to realize I'm taking the rules seriously this time and he gets up, goes to his wardrobe and pulls out a robe which he slips on.

"Well I guess I'll see you tomorrow then," I say when I'm dressed.

Christian nods his head.

"Yes. I'll pick you up around seven thirty. Text me your address," he says.

I nod my head and Christian comes towards me. For a moment, I think he's going to kiss me again, and if he does, I know the rules will go out of the window again. Instead of kissing me on my hungry mouth though, he kisses me on the cheek and I force myself to walk away. If the rules do end up getting broken again – or should I say when the rules inevitably end up getting broken again - it won't be because of me I'm determined to exercise some self control; no matter how hard that might be going to be.

AVA

I stand in front of my full-length mirror and I turn this way and that admiring my new dress. I can't keep the smile off my face whenever I look at it. I still can't quite believe I now own something so beautiful, so exquisite. I feel like a princess in a fairy tale, a modern-day Cinderella where Prince Charming has somehow become my fairy godmother and my knight in shining armor as well as my prince.

I've had my nails done, painted in a dark blue colour to match my dress, the tips finished with silver glitter, and I've had my hair pinned up in a tumbling mass of curls that would have looked like a bird's nest if I'd done it myself but looks sophisticated and neat when my stylist has done it.

I check the time. It's a couple of minutes to seven thirty and I can feel nerves starting to flutter through my stomach. Christian will be here any minute now and while I'm not nervous at the thought of seeing him, I am nervous at the thought of the gala. I just don't know the sort of people who move in the kind of circles that Christian and his father move in. They will literally be the only two people I know at the whole event, and while Mr. Kramer has always been perfectly nice to me, he was only ever seeing me as a legal secretary. I can't help but wonder if he will judge me a lot more harshly now that he thinks I'm his son's girlfriend. And if he does, do I have any chance of making the grade?

The intercom buzzes, pulling me out of my head for a moment. I rush from the bedroom and slip my feet into my high heels and grab my clutch bag which already has some money, a lipstick and my cell phone in it from where I organized it earlier. I walk on through the living room and down the hallway and then I take my keys out of my front door and I step outside of my apartment into the brightly lit hallway and lock the door behind me and then I put my keys in my bag too. I take a deep breath to help to try and steady my nerves as I head to the elevator.

By the time I reach the lobby, I'm no calmer than I was in my apartment, but I have managed to put my game face on, and no one would ever know how nervous I truly am. I cross the lobby and pull the main door open and step out into the street. I smile when I see Christian standing in the street beside the open door of a black limousine.

He looks gorgeous in his formal black suit and white shirt and I feel my nerves melt away, replaced by something much more primal. I take a step towards him and he comes to meet me. He takes my hand in his and kisses the back of it. I smile at him as he looks up from my hand and shakes his head.

"Wow. You look… just wow," Christian says.

"You like the dress then?" I say.

"I love it. You are absolutely stunning," Christian says.

I feel the sexual tension between us like electricity crackling in the air and I know we're going to have to work really hard to keep to our agreement of no sex for a year – a whole fucking year; what were we thinking when we agreed to that?

Christian still holds my hand in his and he leads me to the car. He gestures for me to get in and I do, smiling my thanks to him. He walks around to the other side of the car and gets in and the driver pulls away, heading towards the center of the city.

"You look pretty good yourself you know," I say to Christian after a moment.

"Only pretty good?" Christian says. "Not like off the scale good or anything?"

"Don't push it," I grin.

Christian laughs and shakes his head.

"I see you're going to be one of those high maintenance girls," he says.

"Oh you had better believe it," I laugh.

We arrive at the venue after about fifteen minutes' drive time. It's being held in the ballroom of a fancy hotel, the sort of place I would never be able to afford to stay in. Christian gets out of the limo and hurries around it to get my door for me. I step out onto the red carpet that has been laid out for the event. For a moment, I imagine what it must be like to be famous, getting out of limos onto red carpets all of the time, people screaming your name and taking your picture as you walk. I don't think I'd like that much, but if it had to happen, I'd want it to happen while I was wearing this dress.

159

We slip inside of the hotel and I try not to look too fazed by the extensive, glamourous lobby. It's all white with chrome fixtures and fittings, the ceiling high and the space airy and luxurious. The reception desk is a huge marble topped affair and the seating area opposite it is adorned with plush, crushed velvet sofas.

Christian leads me across the lobby and under an archway to a set of large, glass double doors. He pulls one of them open and gestures for me to enter. I step into the ballroom and look around. It is huge and beautifully decorated in white and gold. It looks almost like it's set up for a wedding with the white and gold streamers across the ceiling, the balloon arches dotted around the place and the white seat covers adorned with golden voile bows.

There are already plenty of people here and I look around at them all. The women are all glamorous and gorgeous, every-thing about them preened to perfection, and once more, I am glad of my dress. I know I look good in it, and I love the way it feels clinging to my body in all of the right places, the silky material like a lover's caress against my skin. Wearing this dress, my arm linked through Christian's as he leads me further into the room, I can almost convince myself I belong here with this crowd. And I know that even if I can't quite convince myself of that, I can convince them it's true.

The truth is though, this is as much of an act as Christian and I and our fake relationship is. Because if I take the dress off, I am not one of them. They are the well to do set, the "in" crowd. And who am I? A secretary from a normal house with a normal upbringing.

"Chris, Ava, how lovely to see you," Mr. Kramer says as he spots us and makes a beeline for us.

He shakes Christian's hand and claps him on the shoulder and then he lightly embraces me and kisses me on each cheek. He grips my upper arms gently and holds me out at arm's length for a second and then he smiles at me.

"Well look at you. You look beautiful," he says.

"Thank you," I reply, feeling myself blushing.

Mr. Kramer flags down a passing waiter and grabs two glasses of champagne from the tray he carries. He hands one to me and one to Christian and then he raises his own glass.

"To you two," he says.

I glance at Christian, hoping my discomfort isn't showing. This is the one part of this arrangement that I really don't like; lying to Mr. Kramer. It just feels wrong. I tell myself it's better this way though. At least he and his wife get to have some peace of mind thinking that Christian has settled down instead of having to constantly be worrying about him. The thought isn't as reassuring as I had hoped it would be, but it's the best thing I've got and so I roll with it.

"Ah here she is," Mr. Kramer smiles, putting his arm around a pretty woman wearing a gorgeous white dress who has come and joined us.

She smiles around at us and Christian moves in and hugs her and kisses her cheek.

"Hey Mom," he says.

Oh, so this is Mrs. Kramer? Even though our relationship is fake, I find myself suddenly nervous at the thought of meeting Christian's mom. She turns to me and gives me a big smile. She takes both of my hands in hers and we kiss each other's cheeks.

"And you must be Ava," she says.

"Yes, that's me," I smile. "It's a pleasure to meet you Mrs. Kramer."

"It's Louisa. And the pleasure is all mine, although you do have rather a reputation to live up to," she says.

"I… I'm sorry. What do you mean?" I stutter.

"Relax, I'm joking," Louisa smiles, her eyes sparkling with mischief just like Christian's do when he's kidding around. "It's just I've heard so much about how lovely you are. If it's not Christian singing your praises, then it's Jeff. And I know you'll never admit it, but I know all of those anniversary presents, birthday presents, the flowers and chocolates on Valentine's day, they were all you. So thank you. You have good taste."

I smile, a little bit uncomfortable. I know Louisa is joking, but I'm not sure if she really does know I bought those gifts and genuinely doesn't mind, or if she thinks her husband is the exception who buys her gifts himself.

"Mom behave yourself," Christian says and they both laugh. "Seriously, you're embarrassing Ava."

"She'll get used to me," Louisa laughs before I can deny it even though it's kind of true. "And when you bring her to the house for dinner, which you must do one evening, I'll dig all of the old photo albums out and it'll be you who I embarrass."

That stops Christian from saying much else, but Louisa and I have a laugh about it. We chat for a few minutes about what Christian was like as a young boy and then the conversation kind of dries up and I'm not really sure what to say next. Christian and Mr. Kramer are deep into a conversation and Louisa and I stand awkwardly smiling at each other for a moment.

They seem to notice that our conversation has faded out and they come up from their own conversation and while I'm still nervous about all of these people milling around, I am actually relieved when Mr. Kramer beckons over a couple who look like they are in their early thirties, hoping the introductions will take some of the awkwardness away. The man who approaches us has dark hair, worn slicked back. His partner has platinum blonde hair and long, fake nails. The pair of them ooze money.

I feel Christian tense up beside me and I glance towards him but other than a slight tightening of his jaw, he looks completely relaxed and normal. I doubt anyone else would have even noticed his momentary tensing up.

"Ava, this is Lewis, Mr. Foley's son. And his fiancé Martha," he says. "Lewis, Martha, this is Ava, Christian's partner. And of course you both know Christian and my wife, Louisa."

"Ava, how are you? It's so good to finally meet you. I've heard so much about you," Lewis gushes, taking my hand in both of his and pumping it up and down while Mr. and Mrs. Kramer greet Martha and Christian looks on.

"I... umm," I falter, unsure of what to say.

The moment to tell him I'm ok has passed by; he didn't pause long enough to allow me to answer that question. And I really don't know what to say to the part where he said that he's heard so much about me, because judging by Christian's standoffishness with the couple, I can't see him having told Lewis much of anything. Lewis laughs and shakes his head as he releases my hand.

"It's ok. You don't have to pretend Christian has spoken about me. I know he's not a big fan of mine," he says with a shrug.

"So how have you heard about me then?" I ask with a frown.

It's probably not the most polite response I could have come up with, but I am genuinely curious and the question just kind of slips out before I have a chance to think it through. For a second, I think I see something in Lewis's eyes. Panic? Shame? I'm not sure and it's gone almost as quickly as it came, that wide charming smile taking its place once more.

"From my dad of course," he says.

I find this damned odd. Why the hell would Mr. Foley, who I barely know, speak to his son about me? I try to shake off the feeling that Lewis has lied to me. I mean I do think he has lied to me, but I don't think it's anything malicious. I think he made a silly, throwaway statement and then when I asked him how he had heard about me, he didn't want to have to admit he lied so he said it was from his dad.

He turns his attention away from me and concentrates on Christian. He slaps him on the shoulder like they are old friends despite just telling me they don't necessarily like each other. I suppose they could be old frenemies.

"Christian, my man," Lewis says. "It's nice to meet your girl-friend. Honestly, if I hadn't seen her with my own eyes, I'd have said she was imaginary. Unless of course she's an escort and you're paying her for her services."

I feel myself blush at his words – they are a little bit too close to the truth for me to be comfortable with them - and Christian glares at Lewis like he might smack him in the mouth.

"Lewis!" Mr. Kramer exclaims. "How disrespectful to Ava."

"Sorry love, no offense," Lewis says, flashing his game show host smile in my direction again. "I just can't imagine a world where a girl like you dates a guy like him without some good reason. I mean it can't be his charming personality or his dashing good looks that attracted you right? Because for it to be that, he would have to have some of one or the other."

I don't know the history between Christian and Lewis or why Christian doesn't like him, but at this moment, I decide I don't much like him either. I turn to Martha and smile sweetly at her.

"Is he always like this or is he just nervous because he's not used to polite company?" I say.

Everything goes quiet for a moment and I hope I haven't gone too far, but then Lewis bursts into laughter and the tension melts away on his laughter.

"Oh I like her," he says, clapping Christian on the shoulder again. "She's definitely a keeper."

"You know it," Christian jokes back.

I'm relieved all the same when Lewis and Martha excuse themselves and move on towards the seating area.

"I'm sorry if I was a little bit rude there," I say, more to Mr. and Mrs. Kramer than to Christian. "He just comes across as kind of smug and it touched a nerve for some reason."

"He's harmless enough. A little immature maybe," Mr. Kramer says. "But if you're worried you offended us, don't be; you didn't. Now if you'll excuse me, I have a few things to sort out still."

"Yes, and I have a thousand and one people to greet," Mrs. Kramer agrees and with that, they both scurry off to do their respective duties.

"You really don't like him, do you?" I say to Christian after Mr. and Mrs. Kramer have walked away and we're sitting down at a table on the edge of a huge dance floor. "Lewis, I mean."

"I hate him." Christian says without hesitation. "And he's the person I will lose my half of the company to if I don't make good on my word to my dad."

"That guy?" I say, screwing my nose up. "Then we had both better make damned sure we get this right because there's no way in hell that I'm working for that douchebag."

Christian laughs and nods his head.

"He's a douchebag alright. You know, I never would have thought of it, but just introducing you to Lewis would have been enough to get you to agree to all of this wouldn't it?" he says.

"Honestly? Yes," I agree. "But it's too late now, we have a deal and you're not wiggling out of it that easily."

"Fair enough," Christian laughs.

Another couple come and join us at our table. Christian introduces me to them – Mark and Maria something or other. When she greets me, I have to bite the inside of my mouth to keep from laughing. When I called Sophie before coming here tonight and told her how scared I was of not being well bred enough for these people, Sophie told me to put on a British accent, saying that it would make me seem exotic and automatically posher than I am. I refused to do it of course, but Maria has a British accent. Has she been taking lessons from a friend like Sophie? Is she as out of place here as I am?

I quite like the idea of having found a kindred spirit, but as the conversation progresses, as nice as Maria is, it soon becomes clear to me that there is nothing fake about how posh she is. She's just finished telling a story about something that happened to her at the royal wedding for goodness sake.

Still, I stand my ground as well as I can, thinking of that horrible man who would get Christian's job if I didn't play my part well enough. It helps that I get to tell them I have been to law school and that I work at a top law firm. I just don't mention the fact that I am only a legal secretary and not a lawyer and the couple seem suitably impressed.

I'm actually starting to relax a little bit and I tell myself that I've blown this up into something it's not when Mr. Kramer gets up on the stage at the front of the dance floor and asks for our attention. He talks for a bit about the charity the gala is supporting and why it's so close to his heart and then he announces the start of the auction. I had no idea there would be an auction, but I've brought like fifty dollars so maybe I can get something and not look too tight.

"The first item up for auction is a two week all inclusive holiday to Marbella for two, valued at five thousand dollars. Who wants to open the bid at three thousand dollars?" he says.

Ok, so they're starting with their show stopper item I say to myself. It's not a big deal. Only two or three people are bidding. It's not like I'm the only one who isn't. The holiday sells for seven and a half thousand dollars. It's more than what it's worth, but it's for charity, that's bound to happen.

"Our next item is a beautiful Cartier necklace," Mr. Kramer says. "This particular piece is the Reflection Du Cartier, it's white gold and diamonds and it's valued at around thirteen thousand dollars."

No one else seems to be in the least bit shocked by this, but I am. Not least because that's an exorbitant amount of money for a necklace, but also because it has just occurred to me that the holiday wasn't the show stopper – the auction is starting with the lower value items first and working up to the show stoppers. Not many people bid on the holiday because they want the better things, not because they couldn't afford it.

The horror must be showing on my face because Christian shuffles closer to me so we can talk without being overheard.

"Hey. Are you alright?" he says.

I nod my head.

"Yes. I… it's just… oh it's nothing," I say.

"It must be something. Talk to me Ava. Tell me what's going on," he says.

"It's just that… well, I don't belong here Christian. In your world. With your inner circle of rich friends. I don't have the sort of money to bid on these items and I don't have the sort of money that would ever allow me access to your social circle if I wasn't on your arm," I blurt out. "Most of these people would look down on me, not view me as someone to socialize with."

"Ok, firstly, with a few exceptions, these people are strangers to me. Most of them are business men and women who are well known for their charity work who my father has invited here for that reason only. A small handful of them are my dad's friends, but they aren't my friends. My inner circle as you call it consists of friends from college and from my old law firm. People like me and you Ava. Normal people. Believe me, I don't feel any more comfortable here than you do. I've just been doing this for long enough that I know how to hide my discomfort with it, that's all," he says.

"Really?" I say. "You're not just saying that to make me feel better are you?"

I can't imagine Christian being uncomfortable in any room with any type of people, but he shakes his head.

"No. Them having money doesn't make them better people than you or me," he says. "And I just try to remind myself of that whenever I'm at one of these stupid events."

I smile at him, not fully convinced he's not just saying it to make me feel better, but realizing I don't really mind if he is. It's still good of him to try and reassure me. Christian squeezes my hand where it rests on the table and after the little reassuring squeeze, he doesn't let go of my hand. I smile at him and turn my hand over, entwining my fingers with his. I don't know if it's just a part of the act, although it seems a bit pointless if it is because his father is up on the stage still doing the auction, but whatever it is, it feels nice and I decide to stop over thinking everything for a while and just try to enjoy the evening for what it is.

I watch the auction, fascinated by the items and by the amount of money people are willing to pay that is well over the odds for the retail value of the items. I suppose that's nice though. It means that they genuinely want to help the charity – or be seen to be helping the charity if you're a bit cynical like me. Either way, the charity wins so that can only be a good thing.

Mr. Kramer smiles out at us, looking around the room, including everyone, pulling us into his words.

"This next item is a personal favorite of mine," he says. He unfurls a poster and holds it aloft. It's the poster for a James Bond movie. "This item is absolutely priceless as I'm sure you can imagine. It's signed by all of the cast. Who wants to start the bidding at two thousand dollars?"

A few hands go up around the room and I watch them. The price is up to sixteen thousand dollars when Christian nudges me gently with his elbow.

"You should bid," he smiles.

"Oh no," I say, shaking my head. "I don't have that sort of money and if I did, I'd want something better than a poster to show for it."

"I don't mean try to win. Just have a bid or two. It'll be fun and it'll push the price up a bit, make some extra money for the charity. Look, there are three people in this bidding war.

Drop out as soon as one other does and you're safe. And if the worst comes to it and you end up winning the auction, I'll pay for the poster and we'll put it up at work in my office or something," he says.

"Are you sure?" I say.

Christian nods his encouragement.

"Do I hear seventeen thousand five hundred?" Mr Kramer says.

Tentatively, I pick up my paddle from the table in front of me and raise it in the air.

"Seventeen five on my right. Do I hear eighteen?" Mr. Kramer says.

Another paddle waves in the air and I raise my own again. This is fun. More fun than I thought it would be, and I can instantly see why people pay over the odds for things in this situation. Yes, it's for charity, but it's more than that. It's like a kind of adrenaline rush wondering if you'll be the one to win the item. I could easily let myself get carried away here, but I remember Christian's advice about when to drop out.

"Twenty-three thousand? Do I hear twenty-three thousand?" Mr. Kramer says.

I raise my paddle and he nods at me.

"Twenty-four thousand?" Do I hear twenty-four thousand?" Mr. Kramer says.

The man I've just out bid shakes his head and my attention turns to the other two bidders as does Mr. Kramer's. They both shake their heads and I feel the color drain from my cheeks. Have I seriously just cost Christian twenty three thousand dollars?

"Twenty-three thousand dollars. Going once," Mr. Kramer says. He pauses. "Going twice."

He looks around and lifts his little hammer, ready to finalize the sale.

"Oh, my God, I'm so sorry," I say to Christian. "I'll find a way to pay you back, I swear."

"Going three times," Mr. Kramer says.

"It's fine Ava, it's only money and it's for a good cause. Relax," Christian says.

Mr. Kramer starts to form the word sold when a voice shouts out from the back of the room.

"Twenty-four thousand," the voice shouts.

"I have twenty-four thousand. Do I hear twenty-five?" Mr. Kramer asks, looking at me.

I shake my head, relief flooding through me. I try to look sad rather than relieved until Mr. Kramer looks away and starts doing his whole going once going twice thing again. I look at Christian and we both laugh and I think he's as relieved as me even though I know he won't admit to it.

"Sold for twenty-four thousand dollars to Lewis Foley," Mr. Kramer announces.

Light applause moves through the room as it has for all of the high-ticket items. I clap along with them and glance at Christian expecting him to be mad. Instead, he's beaming and he's clapping louder than anyone else. When the applause dies down and Mr. Kramer moves onto the next item, I glance questioningly at Christian.

"I thought you'd be annoyed that Lewis got it," I say.

"I would have been if we'd actually wanted it," Christian says. "But we didn't. We basically pushed the price up and Lewis there jumped in and saved us thinking he was shitting on us. It's the second best thing to happen all night."

"What's the best thing?" I ask.

"Seeing you in that dress of course," Christian replies.

I smile at him, giddy from the compliment and the thrill of the auction, and yes, admittedly, from the constant flow of champagne. I really didn't expect to enjoy this night, but I'm starting to and I relax and go with the flow and just let myself enjoy the rest of the night.

CHRISTIAN

I can't believe it but I've actually enjoyed tonight. I've been to a ton of these types of events and they are always stuffy affairs, plenty of networking and schmoozing going on, plenty of showing off how much money people can afford to throw into the ring, but never anything even resembling a good time. And yet tonight, it's been different. And I know exactly why. It's because of her. Ava.

She brings a lightness to me, and somehow, when I'm with her, I can shut the rest of the world out and we can just have a good time in our own little world. After the auction finished, we sat together giggling and whispering like two teenagers, assigning the people around us fake personas and mimicking the conversation that fake persona might be having with the person next to them. We created royalty, spies, pop stars, a housewife with a serious wandering eye, a plastic surgeon and an astronaut. And those are just the ones that I can remember.

Once we got started on that, the conversation between us flowed easily and we have barely come up for air, we've just been talking and laughing the whole night. It's actually starting to become difficult to remember that none of this is real. Although I suppose some of it is real. Like our laughter. That's real. And the way I feel when I am holding Ava, when I'm kissing her, when I'm inside of her feeling her juices coat me as she comes. All of that is real. In fact, the only thing that isn't real is the actual term girlfriend. But I can't think like that, because maybe Ava is just really good at playing her role and when the time is up, she might be able to just happily walk away and I really don't want to get my heart broken. We talked about this. We can't let ourselves get attached to one another. And this is why.

I think we are allowed to acknowledge any misjudgements we may have made about each other though. At least privately if not to one another. When I first met Ava, I thought she was smoking hot and that hasn't changed. But the next morning when she snapped at me for no apparent reason, I thought she was uptight, needy and kind of a prude. She is none of those things. She is honest in a blunt, direct way that makes me want to strangle her sometimes. And she is stubborn when she wants to be. But she's also gorgeous and funny and actually she's quite laid back. And she's smoking hot of course. And she's anything but a prude. And did I mention that she's smoking hot?

I'm kind of tempted to ask Ava about her first impressions of me and whether or not they have changed, but I'm afraid it might lead to her asking me about my first impressions of her and that is bound to end up with us arguing and the last thing I want to do is ruin our evening together by having it end with a fight between us.

There isn't much time left until our limo is booked to take us back home and I really don't want the night to end. There is still one thing we haven't done and now is the time to remedy that. I stand up and hold my hand out to Ava.

"Let's dance," I say.

She raises an eyebrow but she puts her hand in mine and gets up and allows me to lead her to the dance floor where several other couples are dancing. I wrap one arm around Ava's waist and place my other hand on her hip. She hooks an arm around my neck and rests her other one on my shoulder. She smiles up at me as we begin to move.

"You looked surprised when I asked you to dance," I comment.

"I didn't think you'd be the dancing type to be honest," Ava says.

"Well you've learned something new about me tonight then huh?" I say. I grin and lean closer to Ava so I can talk directly into her ear. "Mind you, if I hadn't been drinking champagne all night, you're probably right."

Ava giggles and I smile. I love to make her laugh. I love the way it sounds, musical and sweet, and I love the way it makes her eyes sparkle. I hold her tighter for a moment, and then I take her hand and spin her away from me and pull her back in. She giggles again and then we're both laughing as we spin our way around the dance floor. After a while, Ava leans against me and laughs.

"Oh no more. I'm dizzy," she laughs.

I wrap my arms around her and hold her against me and for a moment, we sway. After a while, I feel Ava's head shifting against my chest and I look down at her. She has lifted her head, her face tilted up to me. She smiles up at me.

"I've had a great time tonight Christian. I didn't think I would, but I have," she says.

"Me too," I tell her. "But the night isn't quite over yet."

I pick up my pace a little and Ava stirs against me. I spin her out again and reel her back in. This time though, when she comes back against my chest, there is no laughter. Her eyes shine but it's with desire rather than laughter. And I can't help myself. Before I know it, I'm leaning down to her, finding her lips with my own. I tell myself it's part of the act that I'm just showing everyone how we are as a couple, but it's a lie. I am kissing Ava because I want to kiss her and that's all there is to it. I don't care who is watching and who sees. It's like at this moment, there is only me and Ava in the whole world.

As I kiss Ava, her hands slide down my chest and move around my sides and onto my back until her arms are wrapped tightly around my waist. I have my arms around her shoulders and I move one hand down her body, caressing her curves. I move my other hand up and cup her face and then I move it back down to her shoulder. I feel the strap of her dress against my fingers, and I almost push it down before I remember myself.

I don't stop kissing Ava though. Even when I remember we're in a room full of people, including my father. My lips tingle where they touch hers. She tastes of champagne and vanilla, a delicious combination that I never want to stop tasting. She is pressed so tightly against me that I can feel the hardness of her nipples pushed against my chest. It's all I can do to keep myself from getting hard as I run my hands down Ava's back. I cup her ass for a second and then I move my hand to her hips. I feel her smile slightly, her lips moving against mine.

We finally come apart and Ava opens her eyes and looks into mine for a second, and I see something there in her eyes at this moment. It's something a lot more powerful than the lust I saw there moments ago. If I'm not mistaken, Ava is looking at me with love shining in her eyes.

The song ends and the lights come up. Ava smiles and steps out of my arms and the look is gone and I'm left wondering if I imagined it there in the first place. I know I should want to have imagined it. I know I should think that a look like that in Ava's eyes is dangerous and messy and makes everything complicated, but despite all of that, I don't. I want to have seen love in her eyes. I want it to be real. Because I want her to feel about me as I am starting to feel about her.

I take her hand in mine and we walk off the dance floor together.

"Our ride will be here any minute," I say. "I'm just going to go and say goodbye to my mom and Dad."

"Oh I'll come with you," Ava says. "I want to say goodbye to them too."

I nod my head and we walk over to my dad's table where he's sitting with my mom and some of their friends. My dad stands up when he sees us approaching.

"We're leaving now Dad, thanks for a lovely evening," I say.

"Yes, thank you Mr. Kramer," Ava echoes.

"Now we're practically family, I think it's about time you started calling me Jeff," my dad says to Ava.

Ava smiles and blushes slightly. She nods her head. My mom gets up and hugs Ava and then me.

"Good night you two," she says. "Ava it's been a pleasure to meet you."

"Likewise," Ava smiles.

"Don't be a stranger, you hear me? Get Christian to bring you over for dinner and to see those photo albums," my mom says.

"Oh, I will. I can't wait to see them," Ava giggles.

I take Ava's elbow and lead her away from my parents towards the lobby and the exit beyond it.

"That's not going to happen, you know that right?" I say with a laugh as we cross the lobby. "I mean we can go to my parents' place for dinner, but I'm burning those photo albums first."

"Spoil sport," Ava laughs.

I look across at Ava as she lays beside me in my bed. Her cheeks are still flushed pink from the orgasm I've just given her and I can still feel the delicious heaviness in my body left behind by my own orgasm. I know we made a rule that we weren't going to do this, but I'm so glad we broke it. Ava is incredible and it's like every time we have sex, it's a little bit better than the last time, and each time I tell myself that's it, it can't get any better than that, but then each time it does.

At some point, sex with Ava is absolutely going to blow my mind if it keeps on getting better like this, but my God will I enjoy myself while I lose myself in her completely. I close my eyes and snuggle against Ava and as I drift away into sleep, I feel truly happy for the first time in as long as I can remember.

AVA

Well here I am again in Christian's bed. It's been roughly thirty hours since we made the no sex rule and we've had sex twice since then. He's asleep now and I don't know what to do, whether I should stay or leave. I want to stay, but I feel like that's breaking another rule, a rule way more serious than the one about us not having sex. I feel like if I stay, I'll get more attached to Christian, but at the same time, I wonder if it's already too late to worry about that, because when I'm not with him, I already miss him and that's not good.

That should be a reason to leave, but I'm making it into a reason to stay. If I already miss him, then surely it's too late to worry about the consequences of getting too attached, so I might as well just stay and enjoy his company for now. Or at least that's the logic I'm working by at the moment.

My cell phone beeps from my clutch bag on the ground distracting me from my thoughts for a moment. I slip out of bed and retrieve my cell phone. The cold air wraps around me making me shiver and I'm relieved when I slip back under the duvet and feel Christian's warmth enveloping me once more. I know at this moment that I'm not going anywhere tonight.

I check my cell phone. The beeping sound was a text from Sophie.

"Are you awake?" her text reads.

"Yes, what's up?" I reply.

"L fucking stood me up. We were meant to be having a Netflix and chill night and he texted me saying he had to work late and that he was sorry but he'd be over later and he hasn't showed up the bastard," Sophie's text says.

I shake my head. I can't believe that. She thought he was the one a couple of days ago and now he has practically ghosted her. I don't get men. I don't get them one little bit. It makes me think Christian is probably right about us – keep it business like, and it won't get messy.

"Babe it's his loss. What an utter dick," I send back.

I know it's a bit generic but I don't know enough about him to tailor a personal insult to him. I don't even know his name, Sophie always shortens everyone to an initial in her texts and that's all I know, and it seems a little insensitive asking her now. Plus, if he's ghosting her, what does it even matter what his name is now?

"I can really pick them," Sophie sends me.

"You know he could have a genuine reason. Maybe he still hasn't finished work. Or maybe he didn't want to call you so late in case you had fallen asleep," I send.

I'm not sure if I believe it or not, but I want to make Sophie feel better and it could be true. I mean there have been nights where I've been at work later than this. I don't know what L does but it's possible he does something where when there's a crisis it's all hands on deck and if you have to stay all night then you do it without complaint.

My cell phone pings again.

"Maybe," Sophie's text reads. "I mean he is a lawyer and didn't you say they often work late?"

"Yes. I've worked later than this myself and I'm just the secretary. If there's a big case, it's not unheard of for the lead lawyers and their associates to work overnight," I reply.

It's funny because I was really only trying to put Sophie's mind at rest and make her feel a bit better about herself, but if this mysterious L is a lawyer, then there's at least a fifty percent chance that it is actually true that he's still stuck at work.

"So what do I do? Will it look desperate if I call him now?" Sophie's next text reads.

"A little bit, yeah. Plus, if he's at work he's not going to be able to take personal calls anyway. The best bet is to go to bed and wait until tomorrow. If he's for real, there's no reason why he won't call you in the morning. And if he doesn't then you were right and he's just a douchebag," I write.

"You're right. Thanks. You've got the right idea. All the fun parts, none of the pain, and you get paid at the end of it. I need to find me a deal like that," Sophie texts.

I send back a laughing emoji but I'm not so sure it's funny. And I'm not so sure it's the right idea either, because the way I'm starting to feel, I know it's going to get messy soon and that's when the fun stops and the pain starts.

Unless…. no, don't even start to go there, Ava, I tell myself. Don't let yourself even imagine for one second that Christian might be getting as attached to you as you are to him. He's just enjoying the no strings sex and he thinks that you are too.

I put my cell phone down on the nightstand and turn off the lamp. I turn onto my side and pull the duvet tighter over myself and close my eyes. Christian mumbles something behind me, his voice thick with sleep and I know he's not really talking to me, he's just half awake. He moves closer to me and puts his arm around me and snuggles into my back and then he's quiet again, his breathing deep and even.

And I know I'm not meant to be going there, but I have to wonder if it's possible. I have to. Because do you really snuggle into someone like this if it's just about casual sex? Or is this a sign that it's more than that between us, or at least that it could be?

I don't even know anymore, but I do know that continually overthinking it isn't going to help me. As I fall asleep, I vow a new rule to myself. I'm just going to take one day at a time and see how things pan out. I'm not going to keep over-thinking everything and I'm certainly not going to do something stupid like blurt out that I'm getting attached to Christian. Sometimes, things are just best left unsaid.

AVA

One Week Later

I wake up and I'm in Christian's bed again. It's become the norm for us now; I've woken up in his bed so many times now, it won't be long before I start to think of it as our bed instead of his bed. The no sex rule has gone so far out of the window I think it's probably in the next state. I haven't been home except for changes of clothes and to collect my mail since the gala.

It's strange because if we were officially dating, I would say we were moving way too fast, but somehow, because we're still telling ourselves this is just business, it seems fine. It's not scary because we're already committed to each other for a year, so what difference does it make if we're together for all of it or just some of it? Or at least that's what I think makes it less scary anyway. Maybe in truth it's just because I want to be around Christian and it's easier to think up other ideas than just admit to the simple truth of that.

Despite all of Christian's reassurances, I'm still a bit worried that I don't fit into his world though. Whether I have feelings for him or not, I have to fit in with his friends and with his family. Because that's part of the deal. We have to be believable as a real couple. And it's even more important if we ever do decide to give a real relationship a try. I don't want to be one of those girlfriends who come into her guy's life and changes everything. I don't want him to feel like he can't see his friends because of me. I don't want them to feel awkward coming to see him at home in case I'm there.

I know I'm getting really far ahead of myself with thoughts of Christian and me being a real couple, but it's early and I'm still half asleep and I seem to be more susceptible to crazy thoughts right before I go to sleep and right when I first wake up. I think it's because my guard is down at those times.

I look over at Christian who is still asleep beside me and some of the anxiety melts away. He has a calming effect on me, because I know that I do fit in with Christian. We have definitely clicked in a way that you just can't fake. I know that much for certain. And I suppose if Christian is telling me the truth – and really, he has no reason at all to lie - and his friends really are just like him, then maybe, just maybe, this could work out after all.

I try to shut my thoughts of where I fit in and where I don't off. Like I said, there's no reason for Christian to lie to me about what his friends are like. It would make no sense. It's not like I'm his girlfriend and he's trying to appease me. It's my job to get this right and he would surely be expected to warn me if his friends were going to be difficult so I could prepare myself for them.

Ok, so I didn't quite succeed in shutting my thoughts off there. I sigh and look once more at Christian's sleeping face and this time when I tell myself to stop overthinking everything, it's a whole lot easier now that I'm focused on Christian. It's so easy to just lose myself in the fantasy of us together and forget about any of the practicalities that could stand in our way. If only.

Christian's eyes flutter open as I watch him and he flashes me a sleepy smile and runs a hand through his hair.

"Good morning," he says in a voice still thick with sleep. He yawns widely. "What time is it?"

"About fifteen minutes before the alarm goes off," I say. "If you want to grab a few more minutes of sleep."

Christian shakes his head and smiles.

"I'd much rather grab this," he says with a laugh.

He reaches out and grabs my hip, pulling me towards him. I laugh with him as I fall against him and end up wrapped in his arms. The laugh cuts out abruptly when his lips find mine. I kiss him back. We share a lazy, first thing in the morning kiss, but despite the laziness of the kiss, I feel my body responding to Christian's and my clit starts to tingle, my nipples hardening and goosebumps popping up on my skin as tingles spread out through my body.

I run my hand down Christian's bare back and cup his ass cheek, pressing him more tightly against me. I lift my leg and hook it over his hip and he slips inside of me and then he pushes me onto my back and begins to pump into me, long, slow strokes that feel delicious in a tingling, teasing sort of way.

I cling to him as he moves his lips from mine and kisses down my neck before resting his head on my shoulder as he thrusts. I thrust with him, my approaching climax spurring me on. I wrap my legs around him, pushing him inside of me deeper and putting extra pressure on my clit.

My orgasm sweeps over me, sending tingles rushing through my body, heat radiating out through my limbs. I cling to Christian as I gasp his name. My pussy tightens and Christian moans, his breath warm on my shoulder. He thrusts into me once more and his climax overtakes him, joining me in mine. He moans my name into my ear, sending a shiver down my spine.

After our orgasms are done and he slips back out of me, we cling to each other for a long moment and then he rolls off me, leaving me feeling the morning chill against my bare skin. I pull the duvet back over me and turn to face Christian. I feel a wash of warmth rush over me as I look at him and in this moment, I can't believe how strong my feelings for him are.

Who would have thought that I would have gone from feeling so humiliated and never wanting to see the arrogant jerk again to being in his bed for the millionth time and seeing that he's not an arrogant jerk at all. Seeing that he's actually warm and kind and generous and someone who I just click with in a way I don't usually click with anyone.

"Well now it's definitely a good morning," Christian says with a grin.

"It sure is," I agree.

He leans in and kisses me again, a tender, almost – dare I say it - loving kiss. I kiss him back and move closer to him. I'm starting to think we're going to have sex again when my cell phone beeps and kind of ruins the moment. Christian pulls back from me.

"It's only a text message, just ignore it," I say.

"It's ok, the alarm is going to go off at any second anyway," he says.

He kisses me on the tip of the nose and the alarm proves his point, going off and startling me. Christian laughs softly at me jumping and then he shuts off the alarm. He sits up and reaches across me and picks my cell phone up from the nightstand. He leans down and kisses me on the forehead and hands me the cell phone.

"I'll go and start breakfast. Come out when you're ready," he says.

"Thanks," I say.

God, could he be any more amazing? I watch him as he crosses the room and grabs his robe from the chair in the corner. He swings it around his shoulders, blocking my view of his perfect ass, and he pushes his arms into the sleeves. He turns back and smiles at me as he leaves the room. Once he's out of sight, I turn my attention to my cell phone. The text message is from Sophie.

"So L and I are done," it reads.

My eyes open wider for a moment in shock. They seemed to be back on track after he stood Sophie up on the night of the gala. It turned out he was working late and just didn't want to risk waking Sophie by calling her when he finished working at around two am. But obviously something else has happened now. Sophie isn't usually one for being a drama queen so I think it has to be something more than another similar incident. I start typing out a reply to her.

"Why? What's happened?" I write.

I sit and wait for Sophie's reply, enjoying the warmth of the duvet around me, the softness of the pillows beneath my head. I don't have to wait long before my cell phone beeps again.

"The bastard is engaged to someone else. Like I was his mistress or some shit without even knowing it. He's never worked late I bet. That's what he's told me when he can't get away from her. Dick head he is. He actually told me he'd enjoyed our bit of fun but it had to stop. I fucking hate him. HATE him!" Sophie's message says.

My eyes widen again. Like what the fuck? How did he not think to mention to Sophie the fact he was engaged at the beginning of their time together. Because it's really not just a bit of fun if one person is getting attached. And it's also really not just a business arrangement if one person is getting attached, a little voice whispers inside of my head. I ignore it. This isn't about me and Christian. It's about my best friend being shit on and I need to be there for her and make sure she's ok, not turn this around to be about me.

"Forget him. You deserve better," I text back.

I know it's generic but what else can I say? What's done is done and Sophie genuinely does deserve better. Her reply pings in a couple of seconds later.

"Do you want to know the worst part about it? I told him about you and Christian and your arrangement and he seemed to think that was terrible, Christian deceiving his dad like that, and the whole time he was deceiving me and cheating on the poor girl that's actually going to end up stuck married to the lying cheating bastard," her message says.

I can almost feel the anger coming off her through her words, and while I obviously want to be the supportive best friend, I can't help but focus on the part where she's told this guy who is a stranger to me everything about me and Christian. It feels a bit off and I can't help but ask her about it. I mean that's not making it about me. She's the one who brought it up.

"What the fuck Soph? Why were you talking to L about Christian and me and our arrangement? I told you that in confidence. What if he decides to make trouble for us?" I say.

"Why would he?" Sophie's response comes in fast. "He doesn't even know you."

Well no he doesn't but Sophie can be fiery and I have a feeling she's not just going to let this one lie. What if the thing with Christian and me is the only thing Sophie has told him that could be used against her? I know I'm just being paranoid and I sigh and shake off my anger. I go to respond to Sophie but she's already typing another message so I wait a second to see what it says.

"It was just an interesting situation that's the only reason it came up. Besides, he has no reason to want to make trouble for anyone. It's not like I'm about to hunt down his fiancé and tell her the truth. Unless he gives me a reason to," the message says.

Ok, it doesn't sound like Sophie is going to cause trouble. She's had time to think it through and decided against it obviously. That's good.

"Fair enough," I reply. "I'm probably just being paranoid, but please don't tell anyone else about this thing with Christian and me ok?"

"I won't. I know what in confidence means you know," Sophie's next message says.

Do you? I think it, but I don't say it. I know Sophie didn't mean any harm by telling L about us. Like she said it was just something a bit different, something interesting to talk about. And it's not like she told anyone that knows either of us.

Sophie's next reply is almost instantly after her first one.

"I have to get ready for work now. Drinks this weekend?" the second message says.

I want to say no because I really want to spend the weekend with Christian, but I remind myself that Sophie is my best friend and she's just been shit on. She needs me and of course I will be there for her. If you can't rely on your best friend to go out and have fun with you when you've just had your heart broken, then who can you rely on?

"Sounds good," I text back.

I put my cell phone down on the bed beside me for a moment while I think. Yes, L is a bastard, and truthfully, what he did to Sophie doesn't really compare to what Christian and I are doing. There have been no lies between us; we both went into the arrangement with our eyes wide open where Sophie really thought that her and L were going somewhere. But despite the fact that we both went into this with total honesty about what it was, I have been lying recently. To Christian and to myself by insisting that I can keep doing the no strings sex thing. I can't do it. I just can't.

My feelings for Christian are already too strong to keep on doing this without ending up getting hurt, and while we do keep doing it, they are only going to get stronger. I know I have to come clean with him. I won't be the one to mess this thing up. I will stick to the arrangement as I promised I would, but I will insist that we follow the no sex rule now. I'm sure Christian will understand. He might be a little pissed off at first that the amazing, no strings sex has to end, but ultimately, I really don't think he wants me to get hurt.

With a wide yawn, I push myself up into a sitting position. I push the duvet back and get up quickly before I can change my mind and just stay there in the warmth. I go to the chair in the corner and pull on Christian's spare robe. I have a fair few pieces of my own here now – clothes, underwear, toiletries, makeup, hair dryer, all the essentials really – but I like wearing Christian's robe. I like the fact that it still smells of him.

I open the bedroom door and instantly smell the delicious smells of bacon cooking and coffee brewing. My stomach is growling by the time I reach the open plan area where Christian stands in the kitchen section, his back to me, whistling to himself as he cooks. I go over to the dining table and pull out a chair. Christian smiles at me over his shoulder.

"Do you want some coffee?" he asks.

"Please," I say. I start to stand up. "I'll get it though, you're busy. I didn't realize it was ready."

"Sit down, it's fine," Christian says.

He grabs the coffee pot and pours out two large mugs of the coffee. He adds cream to both cups and then he adds sugar to mine and then he comes over to the table and puts mine down in front of me and his in front of the chair next to me. He goes back to the pan full of sizzling bacon.

"So the text message was Sophie, my best friend," I say. "I'm going to go out with her this weekend for drinks if that's ok with you."

"Fucking hell Ava. You don't need my permission to go out with your friends," Christian says.

"I know. I just meant there's nothing planned, is there? Like any event we have to be seen together at?" I say.

It's only when Christian shakes his head that I realize that I'm a little bit disappointed that there's nothing planned for us over the weekend. As much as I want to be there for Sophie, I really want to spend every moment with Christian and if there was a reason I had to be with him, Sophie would have understood that it was like a work commitment and not felt like I was blowing her off. There's no way I can put her off to sit in Christian's apartment.

Christian finishes cooking and he comes to the table with a plate with a huge pile of bacon on it and some fresh crusty biscuits. He goes back to the fridge and comes back with butter and a couple of knives and plates. I take a roll, cut it open and butter it as Christian nibbles on a piece of bacon. I take a couple of pieces of the bacon and put it in the roll and then I sit and eat it, sipping my coffee between each bite. I look out of the window at the view of the city, barely daring to look at Christian knowing that I need to tell him that we can't do this anymore and yet not wanting to ruin the moment. What if this is the last time we are this relaxed together? What if every part of us being in each other's company becomes a part of the act? I would hate that but if that's what being honest leads to, then what else can I do?

"Are you ok Ava?" Christian asks. "You've been quiet since you spoke to Sophie. Has something happened with her or something?"

"Well yeah actually. The guy she was dating turned out to be engaged, but that's not why I'm quiet. I was just thinking," I say.

It's time to be honest with Christian and while I'm dreading it, I know it's for the best. Surely it's better to get my heart broken now than it would be to cling on until further down the line and get it broken later when I'm even more attached to him.

"What were you thinking about?" Christian asks me gently.

I don't think he knows what's going on in my head right now, but I do think he knows it's something quite serious. He looks a little bit worried and it's all I can do not to reach out and squeeze his hand and tell him not to look worried, it's nothing. But I can't. If I chicken out of this conversation this time, I don't think it will ever happen and now that I've come this close, I have to say it.

"Us," I say. I put my half eaten sandwich down on the plate, my appetite pretty much gone now. And I don't really think that has anything to do with the fact that I've eaten. I pick up my cup and sip my coffee and then I put the cup down too. Christian doesn't try to interrupt my silence or push me to say anything further. He just watches me, and finally, I turn to look at him. "The sex has to stop."

"Ok," he says with a grin.

I shake my head and keep my expression serious rather than the usual playful expression we both wear when we talk about stopping the sex between us, and the grin on his face starts to fade.

"I'm sorry Christian, I mean it. The sex has to stop. And this. All of this. It all has to stop," I say, gesturing around me as I speak.

I'm horrified to find that I'm close to tears and I stop talking before the sound of my voice breaking is obvious. So much for just being calm and stating this as a fact and going back to a business deal. Instead I'm on the verge of tears. I'm going to show myself up and Christian won't even want to do business with me after this let alone anything else.

"Hey calm down Ava, it's ok," Christian says, his face a frown of concern. "What is it? What happened?"

He reaches for my hand and I pull it away from him, knowing that if he's kind to me it will only make this even harder to do. I shake my head and pause for a moment, swallowing away the huge lump in my throat.

"It's not ok, Christian," I say. "I'm sorry, but it's not. This was only ever meant to be a business arrangement and we said from the beginning that it could always go back to that if we needed it to and well… I need it to."

"I don't understand," Christian says. "Have I done something to upset you or make you angry at me?"

"No, just the opposite," I say with a sad smile.

"So you're not angry or pissed off with me? You're not upset? But the arrangement that seems to have been working perfectly fine for us suddenly has to stop with no explanation?" Christian says. "And you don't see why I would assume that I have somehow upset you."

"You haven't upset me," I shout. "For fuck sake Christian. I'm not doing this because I don't want to be around you. I'm doing this because I can't bear the thought of not being around you. I've tried to switch my emotions off. I really have. But I can't do this anymore. I can't make it harder and harder for myself."

"What are you saying Ava?" Christian says.

"I'm saying that I'm in love with you and I know that wasn't part of the deal and I don't expect you to do anything about it and..." I shout.

Christian cuts me off by grabbing the lapels of the robe and pulling me towards him and kissing me hard on the mouth. For a moment, I resist his kiss and try to pull my head away from him, but he holds on and a second later, I can't resist him any longer and I'm kissing him hungrily, already regretting telling him that this has to end.

Finally, we break apart, both of us slightly breathless. I search Christian's face as we watch each other. After a second, he smiles.

"I love you too Ava," he says.

"I... what?" I say, sure I've misheard him.

"I love you too," he repeats.

I shake my head, refusing to let myself believe that this could be true, refusing to set myself up for more pain.

"You don't have to pretend Christian. I said I would do this for a year and I will. I'm a big girl, I can handle my feelings. Please don't patronize me," I say.

"I'm not patronizing you," Christian says quickly. "Honestly Ava, does any of what we have together feel like a business deal to you? Has it ever felt that way?"

I pause and I think about what he's saying. Like, I really think about it. And he's right. At no point have I ever really felt like any of this was fake. I shake my head slowly and look down at the table. Christian goes silent, waiting until I look up and meet his eyes once more.

"I vowed I was never going to tell you this, but what the hell," he says. "Do you remember the day I called you into my office and asked you to be my fake girlfriend?"

I nod my head and Christian goes on.

"We'd spent the night together the night before and I was more than just attracted to you by then. Like it was more than just physical I mean. I already had real feelings for you. And before my dad dropped his bombshell that he'd seen us kissing and everything sort of ran away with me, I had planned to ask you out. Like on a proper date not into a fake relationship," he says.

"Really?" I ask.

Christian nods his head.

"Yes, really," he says.

"So why didn't you?" I ask.

"Because I really was scared it would all get complicated and I didn't want to mess up with the company," he says. He looks away from me for a moment and gives a soft laugh and shakes his head and then he looks back at me. "And honestly Ava? I didn't think you would say yes anyway so I figured I might as well ask you for the thing I believed there was a chance I could persuade you to do."

"I would have said yes to a date with you," I say.

"Well yeah, I know that now," Christian laughs. His laughter fades and he's serious again. "So what happens with us now?"

I shake my head and shrug my shoulders helplessly.

"Honestly? I don't know," I say. "It's not like I have experience with this kind of thing. It's not every day a business deal turns to love."

"I don't know how any of it is supposed to work myself. But I do know this; I don't want to lose you Ava," Christian says.

I feel a warm glow inside of me. Never in my wildest dreams did I expect Christian to say that he felt the same way about me when I confessed my feelings to him. Now he has, I just want him to wrap me up in his arms and never let me go. I know we have to have this conversation, have to work out where we go from here, but I would much prefer we just held each other, kissed each other, made love to each other, and kept the hard part for later.

"I don't want to lose you either," I say. "But I can't be your real girlfriend and be paid to be your fake one at the same time. It's too icky and weird. So if we're going to be together, then we'll have to call the deal off. If we do that, can you handle the messy parts?"

"Yes," Christian says without hesitation. "With you, I think even the messy parts will be amazing."

"I don't know about that," I grin.

"Oh I do," Christian grins. "But wait. Are you sure you're cool to just abandon the deal? Like I'm still getting what I wanted out of it. Are you honestly willing to lose that much money?"

I nod my head. I don't care about the money. Not anymore. I care about Christian. The money was only ever a bonus when this was a business deal.

"I'm sure," I say.

Christian stands up and holds his hand out to me. I slip my hand into his and he helps me to my feet and then pulls me against him and wraps his arms tightly around me. I hold him, my head pressed against his chest and I take a deep breath, relishing the scent of him. He kisses the top of my head.

"God I love you so much," he whispers.

I tilt my head back and we kiss, a hungry kiss, full of passion and yes, now I can say it; full of love. As Christian's tongue creeps into my mouth and massages my own, I move my hands to the front of his body. I untie his robe and push it down his arms. He releases his grip on me long enough to allow the robe to fall to the ground and then he pushes his hands into my hair, his kiss intensifying.

I run my hands over his bare chest and then I wrap one arm around him. The other hand moves lower, skimming over Christian's belly and then I keep moving it, going lower still. I wrap my fist around his huge, already hard cock and begin to move it up and down, my grip firm enough to make Christian moan into my mouth.

He moves his hands out of my hair and down over my body. He lifts up the robe I'm wearing and cups my ass cheeks and lifts me. I allow myself to be lifted and Christian turns and sits me on the dining table where we have just had breakfast. I keep my grip on his cock, still working him. He opens the robe and pushes it down my arms and I release him for a second to free myself of the robe and then I take hold of him again, moving my fist faster now.

Christian runs his hands all over my body and then he cups my breasts and massages them as he leans in and kisses my neck. I put my head back, letting him get to the sensitive skin there and he runs his tongue down my neck and over my shoulder. I moan his name and then his mouth is on mine again, and his hand circles my wrist and moves my hand from his cock.

He nudges my knees further open and I slide to the edge of the table. I feel the top of his cock rubbing around my pussy, teasing me, and then he pushes inside of me, making me gasp into his mouth as he slides in. When he's all the way in, he cups my ass again and I wrap my legs around his waist and my arms around his shoulders as he carries me to the nearest wall and slams me up against it. He runs his fingers along my arms and lifts them from around his neck. He lifts them high, pushing them against the wall and then he holds my wrists in place there with one hand.

He's still pumping into me as his lips find mine once more and his free hand pushes between us and rubs over my clit. I almost come there and then but I hold myself back, wanting to draw it out and make my climax even more amazing when it does hit me.

I can't hold back for long though. My senses are overwhelmed with Christian's touch as he fills me and kisses me simultaneously and my orgasm bursts forth, slamming through me and setting my body on fire. I pull my mouth from Christian's, pressing my face into his neck as I cry out over and over again as the pleasure consumes me entirely.

I'm just beginning to come back to myself when Christian explodes inside of me, moaning loudly as he comes. He keeps me pinned in place as his cock goes wild inside of me, and his back goes rigid. Finally, it's over and a warm feeling of satisfaction envelopes me as Christian carries me away from the wall and takes me over to the sofa where he sits down heavily and holds me on his lap as we gasp for breath. My body is shaking as I come back to myself and where my head is resting against Christian's chest, I can feel his heart pounding in his chest.

His cock stirs beneath me after a few minutes, already hard and ready for me once more, and I pull back enough to smile at him and nod down at his lap.

"You know if we make use of that, we're going to be late for work," I say.

"We'll say we had a working breakfast," Christian says with a grin.

CHRISTIAN

I can't believe how close I came to losing Ava this morning. And the irony is it wasn't because she didn't want to be with me but because she did want to be with me. I can't help but keep on imagining what might have happened if we hadn't talked when we did. Ava would have walked away and I would have always thought she had just gotten sick of having sex with me. I would have then tried to keep my distance and she never would have known I felt the same way about her as she does about me. We would have lost each other before we had even really found each other. It doesn't bear thinking about.

I honestly feel like the happiest man alive as I stand up with Ava in my arms. I don't even care now about the arrangement. I care about her. If our relationship goes wrong, I won't be worried about losing the company, I will be worried about losing her. But it won't go wrong. I'll do everything I can to make damned sure of it.

"Where are you taking me," Ava giggles as I walk across the living room.

"Well if we're going to be late for work anyway, I thought we might as well make the most of it," I say.

I take her to the bathroom and when we're in it and the door's been kicked closed behind me, I finally set her down on her feet. I lean into the shower and get the water going. I stay outside of the shower with one hand inside of it until I get the pressure and the temperature just right.

"M'Lady," I say, standing to one side and gesturing grandly for Ava to enter the shower first.

She giggles again and she steps in. She moans as the water caresses her shoulders.

"Oh that feels so good," she says, her voice breathy, almost a sigh.

I feel my already hard cock hardening some more and I step into the shower with Ava and pull the door closed. She's right; the water does feel good, but it doesn't feel anywhere near as good as Ava looks. She stands facing me, her hair slicked back, her face and body covered in drips of water. She smiles at me and I bend down slightly and kiss her. As I kiss her, I reach to the small shelves in the side of the shower and grab my shampoo.

I pull back from Ava and rub some into my hair and then I squirt out some more and begin to lather Ava's hair. She turns around so her back is to me and I massage the shampoo onto her head, running my fingers through her hair and rubbing her temples. I pull her back ever so slightly when I'm done shampooing her hair and I rub it vigorously as she stands beneath the spray of the water. When her hair is all rinsed, I rinse my own and then I pick up my shower gel and squirt that into my hand.

I rub it over Ava's shoulders, massaging her. I can feel her relaxing under my touch. I rub down her arms, over her back, over her ass cheeks. I turn her back to face me and I soap my hands up again and then I begin to massage Ava's breasts. Her nipples stand to attention beneath my slick palms and Ava moans as I roll each nipple between my fingers. I move my hands lower, down her belly and then I slip one hand even lower, pushing my fingers between Ava's lips and finding her clit.

She gasps as I massage it. I can feel it pulsing against my fingers, getting itself ready for Ava's orgasm. I keep working her until I know she's about to come and then I spin her again so she's facing away from me. I run my hand between her thighs and over her mound from behind her. I can feel how wet she is and I know that Ava is as ready for this as I am.

She leans forward, bracing herself on her palms against the shower wall. She sidesteps with one foot, opening her legs, opening herself up to me. I run my fingers over her mound again and then I slam into her as I begin to massage her clit, my touch hard and fast to match my thrusts.

I love the way Ava feels around my cock, her pussy warm, tight, wet. I love the way she moves with me, her enthusiasm for sex unrivalled by anyone I have ever known. I love the way her body shudders as her orgasm takes her, the way her pussy clamps tightly on me as she moans my name. I love the way she throws her head back as her body tenses up. I love the way she makes me orgasm in a way I never even imagined was possible.

Fire flies through my body as Ava's pussy clenches around me now and sends me hurtling to my climax. I reach over

Ava, resting one hand against the wall of the shower as I come hard. My climax seems to go on forever, but yet still, when it's over, I'm already craving more.

Ava straightens up as I slip out of her and I hold her against me. I kiss her neck and move my hands over her stomach and caress her breasts. She leans back against me and turns her face up to the shower spray for a moment and then she takes my hands in hers and gently pushes my arms to my sides. She turns around and kisses me, a soft, fleeting kiss that tastes ever so slightly of shower gel.

"We're never going to get to work at this rate," she grins. "It's alright for Mr. Managing Partner, no one will dare to question you about where you've been."

"Like anyone would dare to question my legal secretary either," I grin back.

I know technically I'm right. There isn't a chance in hell anyone would have a go at my legal secretary about her hours because her working schedule is none of their business. Still though, I know where Ava is coming from. I know that people in the office are already talking about us being a thing and if I've heard stuff, no doubt Ava's heard stuff too. Some of the partners were at my dad's charity gala and I'm guessing that's where the story about Ava and me being together came from.

She will want to be on her best behavior now because she won't want anyone thinking she's taking liberties because she's with the boss. The funny thing is, when it was just an arrangement between us, I know for a fact that Ava would have gone into work late if I'd convinced her that I wanted us to hang out or whatever, and I know in that situation, she couldn't have cared less what anyone thought of her. Now, our relationship is real though, somehow, and I have a feeling that she does care what people think. It's probably a case of her own integrity. When it was a business arrangement between us, technically she was working when she was with me. Now though, she would just be goofing off. And maybe she doesn't care so much what other people think, but maybe she cares herself, like she wants to remain the professional at work.

Despite understanding Ava's logic on the situation, I still don't want her to get out of the shower and leave me just yet. I hold her against me and kiss her again. She kisses me back, and right at the point where I know if we go any further Ava won't be going anywhere, she pulls back from me. She smiles and quickly turns away and pulls the shower door open. She grins over her shoulder at me and then she steps out and pushes the door closed again behind her.

I watch her silhouette through the frosted glass of the shower as she stands at the sink and brushes her teeth and then she wraps herself in a towel and she's gone from the bathroom and even though I know she's only in my bedroom drying her hair and applying her makeup I miss her already. I shut the water off and step out of the shower.

I stand at the sink that Ava has just vacated and shave and brush my teeth. I use the toilet and then I go through to the bedroom. Ava's been out into the dining area and grabbed the robe she's claimed as her own. She's wearing it now, the towel she had wrapped around her folded up and draped over the chair where the robes usually go, as she perches on the end of my bed applying her makeup. Her hair is already dry.

I open the wardrobe and pull out my clothes for the day – the usual, a suit and a shirt and tie. I get some underwear out and then I dress quickly. I find some socks and put them on and then I slip my feet into my shoes. By the time I'm dressed, Ava has finished putting on the makeup and she has her underwear and a pencil skirt on. She reaches into the wardrobe for her shirt and I cross the room to her.

I wrap my arms around her from behind and kiss her neck. She laughs and swats me away, playfully ducking away from me as she puts on the white shirt.

"Stop it," she laughs. "We've just showered. And we really do need to get to work."

"Yes boss," I say, giving Ava a salute.

She rolls her eyes and buttons her shirt up and then she steps into her shiny black heels.

"I can't wait until today is over," I say.

"Why?" Ava frowns. "You don't have any horrible client meetings or anything scheduled today do you?"

"No, no. Nothing like that," I say. I grin at her. "I just can't wait to get you back out of those clothes, that's all."

She laughs and shakes her head.

"Pervert," she says.

"You love it," I reply.

"I know," she laughs.

We leave the bedroom and as I pick up my keys and wallet and Ava looks for her things and puts them in her purse, a plan starts to form in my mind. It's a plan that leaves me both nervous and excited in equal measure. I don't know really if it's a good idea or not, but I know I'm going to do it. God, I hope it's a good idea.

"Ava?" I say. She looks up from where she's going through her cell phone. "Would you mind taking your own car into the office this morning? I just remembered that I have a few errands I need to run before I get into work."

"Yeah sure," she says. I walk over to her and give her a kiss goodbye. She smiles as I pull back. "Don't miss me too much."

"Oh, but I will and you know I will." I laugh.

CHRISTIAN

I still can't believe I told Ava how I feel about her. Not only that, but I really can't believe she didn't laugh at the very idea of being with me or run away without looking back or do any of the things I'd dreaded. Instead she told me that she feels the same way about me. Never in my wildest dreams did I imagine she might actually love me back. I'm still not quite sure how someone like Ava, an amazing woman, falls for someone like me, but I don't want to question it too much in case Ava starts to question it too and realizes she's being crazy.

Instead of focusing on Ava realizing I'm really not all that much of a catch, I turn my focus back to my plan. The plan I started coming up with makes me feel slightly queasy but mostly in a good way.

I can't help but smile to myself as I think about how things have changed for the better over the last few weeks for me. And the irony is, I kind of owe my happiness with Ava to my dad. If he hadn't made his stupid condition for me to find a girl to settle down with in order to take over his half of the firm, I wouldn't have gotten close enough to Ava for anything to develop between us. Yet when my dad first gave me his condition, I was so angry. Now I'm grateful. Maybe he really does know me better than I think he does. Maybe he even knows me better than I know myself. Maybe he could see something in me, something that told him that with a little nudge and the right person, maybe I was ready to settle down after all. Or maybe not. Maybe he just didn't want me to keep partying and not growing up, but either way I'm grateful to him for his stupid condition.

I'm still smiling to myself by the time I park my car in the mall parking lot and get out. I head for the doors and step inside. Even this early, the mall is bustling with people and I give up trying to hurry and just go with the flow, walking slowly, looking into store windows as I go. Unfortunately, my slow pace gives me time to wonder once again if this is a crazy idea.

When the idea first came to me, I was confident it was a good idea, but now I'm starting to think it's a bad idea. I feel like, if I get this wrong, it will make things too uncomfortable between Ava and me and I'll lose her. But now that the idea is in my mind, I can't quite shake it. I know what I need to do. I need to stop overthinking things and go with my gut. And I'm here because when the idea first came to me, my gut told me it was a good one.

I reach the store I want to go into. A jewelry store. I stand and look at the displays in the window for a moment. I spot a beautiful gold bracelet with jade stones that I think Ava would love. That's it, I tell myself. I can get her something like that. It will be a nice surprise but it won't be too much too soon. I nod to myself, my decision made.

I go into the store to ask to see the bracelet. The store is quiet with soft music playing and the air conditioner makes it the perfect temperature. Three assistants stand behind the glass display cabinets that make up their counter. One is talking to a customer already. The other two are talking to each other but they stop when they see me and one of them steps forward.

"Hi there. I'm Karen. Can I help you with anything today?" she says.

I open my mouth to ask her if I can see the jade bracelet.

"I'd like to see your diamond engagement rings please," I hear myself say.

Somehow, the tranquillity in the store has renewed my confidence and I'm once again sure this is the right move to make. Ava loves me; she said so herself. We want to be together so why not make it official? It's not like we have to get married tomorrow or anything.

"Of course sir," Karen says.

She smiles at me, a wide smile that looks natural rather than a customer service smile. She moves towards a different display cabinet and opens it up. Her body blocks my view of what she's doing, but she's only there for a second or two and then she steps back and closes and locks the cabinet and turns back to where I wait at the counter. She smiles and puts a black velvet ring cushion down on the counter top between us.

I glance down at the rings and instantly I spot the one I just know Ava will love. I point to it.

"That one please," I say.

The ring has a large diamond but it's not so large as to be distasteful. The diamond is set in a cluster of emeralds and the stones are all set into a pretty gold band.

"This one is eighteen carat gold featuring a one carat diamond set into a bed of eight emeralds," Karen says. "It's fourteen thousand, nine hundred and ninety-nine dollars and ninety-nine cents. We carry sizes 4 through 8 in the store or we can order one in if needed."

I nod my head, disappointment swelling up in me. Karen must be able to see it in my face because she smiles sadly and then points to a different ring.

"This one is very similar and it's actually on sale right now," she says.

"It's not the price," I say. "That's not a problem at all. It's the size. I wanted it to be a surprise but now I'm scared I'll get the wrong size."

"Oh don't worry about that. I can help you with choosing the right size," Karen smiles. "And once you've given your girl-friend the ring, if it's a little bit too loose or a little bit too tight, you can pop back in and we will happily resize it for you for free."

"Thank you," I say, feeling myself smiling so wide that my face aches slightly.

It's good news but that's not why I'm smiling so wide all of a sudden. It's hearing Karen refer to Ava as my girlfriend that has made me so happy. I mean of course she's going to say that, but it still sounds so nice to hear it out loud for the first time like that.

"Now, would you say your girlfriend's fingers are bigger, smaller or about the same as yours?" Karen says.

I look at my hand and think about how small and delicate Ava's hand feels in mine.

"Smaller," I say without hesitation. "Way smaller."

"Let me see your hand," Karen says. I place my hand on the counter and she looks at it and nods. She places her own next to it. "And would you say your girlfriend's fingers are bigger, smaller or about the same size as mine?"

"Maybe a little bit bigger," I say.

"Rose, come over her a second please," Karen says over her shoulder and the other assistant comes over.

She smiles when she sees my choice of ring.

"Lucky lady," she says.

"Oh believe me, I'm the lucky one," I tell her.

She smiles again and Karen asks her to put her hand on the counter like we did which she does. Looking at Rose's hand, I really think that it's pretty much the same size as Ava's and I tell the women that.

"I'm a 5 on my engagement finger," Rose says.

She flashes us another smile and then she turns and walks away leaving Karen to finish her transaction.

"Would you like to have a look at the ring in size 5?" Karen asks.

I nod my head and thank her and she takes the little ring cushion away and locks it back in its cabinet and then she goes through a door into what I assume is the storeroom. She's gone for a couple of minutes and then she's back again with a small box in her hand. She opens it and takes out the ring. I take it from her and look at it. I think it looks to be about the right size and I smile and nod and hand the ring back to Karen.

"I'll take it please," I say.

She moves over to the cash register and rings it up. I pay on my card and I leave the proud owner of a tiny box with a huge meaning. I turn and head back towards the parking lot where I parked my car. I'm almost back to it when a travel agency catches my eye and I smile to myself. Wouldn't it be nice to surprise Ava with a weekend away and then propose to her while we're there? It would be way better than just taking her for dinner in a nice restaurant to do it which had been my initial plan.

I don't hesitate about this one. I'm not nervous about asking Ava to go on a weekend trip with me. I know she'll love the idea of it, especially because it will mean there's no chance of me having to pop into work for a bit on the weekend.

I have a look at a few brochures and speak to one of the staff members and before too long has passed, I've booked a weekend in Las Vegas for us for this coming weekend. There's a spring in my step for sure as I head back to my car. I know Ava is going to be so excited about the weekend and I know she'll love Las Vegas – who wouldn't, there's something for everyone there. She'll love the sights and the sounds, the atmosphere, the lights, everything. And hopefully my asking her to marry me will be the perfect end to the perfect weekend. I know it will be for me – well at least it will be if she says yes.

By the time I'm back in my car and moving again, it's almost the time I would have been leaving the office for a meeting anyway and so I change directions and head straight there. The meeting goes well and I sign a new client who is going to bring plenty of business my way and I take that as a sign that good things are coming to me.

By the time I get back to the office parking lot, its lunch time and I sit in my car and text Ava to see if she's free to go and grab some lunch with me. She replies quickly saying that she is free and starving. I smile to myself and then I get out of the car and go to wait at the front of the building for her. I don't have to wait long before I see her coming across the lobby towards the doors. God she's gorgeous. How the hell is she mine?

I smile as she comes outside. She smiles back and then I take her hand in mine and lead her down the street towards the little sandwich bar I know she likes.

"What's going on?" she asks as we walk.

"Umm, we're going to have lunch," I say, not sure what she means. "You're starving, remember?"

She rolls her eyes and digs me with her elbow.

"Alright Mr. Sarcasm," she laughs.

"I'm not being sarcastic. I genuinely don't know what you mean," I say.

She can't know. She can't possibly know about the ring in the glove compartment of my car and what it signifies.

"You just seem happy. But like excited happy," she says.

"I'll go back to being miserable then shall I?" I say.

"Well at least when you are your normal, miserable self I know what's going on," Ava teases me.

I laugh and shake my head. I put my spare hand to my chest.

"That hurts me right here," I say.

We both laugh. As we continue walking, I can feel Ava's eyes on me. She keeps giving me sideways looks and I know I'm grinning like a Cheshire cat but I can't help myself. Ava is right. I am happy. And I am excited happy.

We reach the sandwich place and I grab the door for Ava. She smiles at me and steps in.

"The usual?" I ask.

"Please," she says.

"Ok, grab us a table while I order," I say.

I go up to the counter and order Ava's usual – a chicken salad on rye bread with a diet soda – and my usual – roast beef with mustard on white bread and a black coffee. I pay and grab the tray with our food and drinks on it and turn around. I spot Ava sitting at a table by the window and I head over to her. I hand her the sandwich and her drink and I put my sandwich and drink down on the table for a moment and then I take the tray back to the counter so it's not in our way. I head back to the table and sit down.

Ava has unwrapped her sandwich while I've been gone and she smiles at me and starts nibbling on the end of it while I open mine.

"Oh," she says suddenly. "Of course. That's it."

I look at her waiting for her to go on.

"Your meeting went well I take it? That's why you've been grinning so much," she says.

I really thought I had managed to get control of myself since we got here but apparently that was wrong. I could let Ava think my new found happiness is just to do with the meeting, but I decide to tell her the truth about my excitement. Or at least part of the truth. She looks so pleased with herself for solving the mystery that it seems almost a shame to burst her bubble, but at the same time I know she will be happier about this than the meeting going well.

"The meeting went really well. He signed with us and I can see a lot of business coming our way from him. But that's not why I'm so happy," I say.

"Go on," Ava prompts me. "Spill it."

I pick my coffee up and take a sip and then another.

"Oh come on, it's cruel keeping me in suspense like this," Ava bursts out as I take a third sip of my coffee.

"Well I might have a surprise for you," I say.

"Tell me more," Ava says, leaning closer to me across the table.

"I can't. It's rude to talk with my mouth full," I say and take a big bite of my sandwich.

Ava laughs and shakes her head.

"You are so cruel," she says.

"Only a little bit," I say when I've swallowed my bite of sandwich. "Ok, I'll tell you. I've booked us a little getaway for the weekend."

Ava's face lights up as she smiles with delight.

"Oh really?" she says. I nod my head and Ava claps her hands together. "Oh thank you so much. I can't wait. It'll be good to get away, just the two of us. No work, no one bothering us, just doing what we want to."

"Exactly," I say.

"So where are we off to then?" Ava asks.

"Oh, just a little not well known place called Las Vegas," I say.

"Oh my God," Ava shrieks loud enough that some people at the nearby tables turn to look at us. "How am I meant to contain myself for the rest of the week now?"

"I have no idea but you'll have to find a way," I laugh.

The people who turned to look at Ava must see her excitement because they are smiling at us and I find myself smiling back and in this moment, everything is right with the world.

We finish our lunch and head back towards the office, chatting excitedly at what we are going to see and do while we're in Vegas. I'm glad I decided to tell Ava about this part of her surprise. It's lovely to see her so happy and excited.

We're almost back at our building when Ava's cell phone rings. She fishes it out of her purse and looks at the screen.

"Sorry," she says "I need to take this."

"No worries," I tell her. "I'll be going on up. Thanks for lunch."

"Thanks for Vegas," she grins.

I grin back at her and then I walk towards the building. I hear Ava saying hello as she takes her call and then I'm inside and I can't hear anymore. I cross the lobby and get into the elevator and head up to my floor. As I walk along the corridor towards my office, I'm thinking about what I'm going to do this afternoon. While everything seems to be going just right for me, I decide to take some time to call up a couple of big fish who I would love to land as clients and try to set something up with them.

I push my office door open, already knowing who will be the first person on my call list. I'm whistling to myself as I imagine the moment that he says yes to coming on board as our client and it takes me a moment to realize that there are people in my office.

Of course with Ava out at lunch with me, there is no one around to stop them, but surely common decency says this isn't ok. I realize one of my visitors is my father and then I relax. It doesn't seem so rude since it's him.

"I wasn't expecting to see you today Dad," I say as I half turn to close the office door behind me.

"No, I don't suppose you were," he says.

He sounds kind of angry but I tell myself I'm being paranoid. He has no reason to be angry. If anything, he will be ecstatic when I tell him who I signed this morning. And if I'm wrong and he has a bee in his bonnet over something, then he can just march himself back out of my office because nothing is going to ruin my good mood today.

I turn back into my office and the other man has turned slightly and I realize with disgust that the other man is Lewis Foley. Why the hell my dad has brought the one person he knows I dislike the most in the world to my office is beyond me. Maybe it was to prove that actually, my good mood can be ruined, because it's going that way fast.

"What the hell are you doing here Lewis?" I demand as I walk across my office and go around my desk to take my rightful seat.

"Christian," my dad says, his voice low, a warning.

It's a warning I choose to ignore.

"Yes?" I say. "I'm sorry. Would you rather I be all fake nice to someone I don't like?"

"Well lying seems to be your forte right now so why not," my dad says.

"What?" I demand. "Since when have I been lying to you?"

"Since the moment you told me you and Ava were a thing," my dad says.

I'm taken aback for a moment. Ava and I feel so right now that I can almost let myself forget that we started out as a ruse to fool my father and even once I make myself remember that to be the case, I have no idea how he found out. I decide to leave that on a back shelf for now and go with the absolute truth for now.

"I'm not sure where you got your information from that Ava and I aren't together, but wherever it is, I can assure you it's

IONA ROSE

wrong. Ava and I are very much together. We're even going away together this weekend," I say.

"Drop the act Christian," my dad says. "I know you've been lying to me. Lewis told me everything."

"Oh did he?" I say. I turn my attention to him. "I bet you enjoyed that didn't you?"

Lewis shrugs and gives me a smug smile, the kind that makes me want to punch him right in the mouth. He wipes the smile from his face before my father sees it.

"It brought me no pleasure at all. I just thought Mr. Kramer deserved to know the truth," Lewis says.

"Right. So it had nothing to do with trying to get one over on me then? Or about getting my half of the company?" I demand.

"Oh Christian," my dad says, his tone one of resignation now rather than anger. "Do you really think I would have given away your inheritance like that just because you were still single? I wanted you to find someone and settle down, sure but mostly, I wanted you to stop partying and sleeping around so that you could commit fully to this role. And you were doing that. And now it's all ruined."

"How is it ruined?" I demand. "I have proved myself in the role. I have signed new clients. I've made money for our existing clients. And now you're going to take that away because Lewis came to you with some story?"

"I'm taking it away because you lied to me Christian. And it wasn't a little white lie. It was a huge lie, and if I can't trust you with being honest with me, how can I trust you to run this company honestly?" he says.

I guess then it is possible to have the perfect day ruined because right now, I'm about to lose the firm I have worked so hard for and my father thinks that Lewis Foley is more trustworthy than I am. I'm not sure how we got here but I don't like it one little bit and I'm not about to sit here and just willingly hand over what is rightfully mine.

AVA

I know as soon as I see Sophie's name on my caller ID that she's going to be upset about finding out her dream man was already engaged to someone else. I'm mad on her behalf. I want to find that pig and punch him in the face for hurting my best friend. I take the call.

"Are you ok?" I ask.

"No I'm absolutely fuming," Sophie replies. "Not only did the bastard forget to mention he was already taken, he didn't even tell me his real name."

"Huh?" I say. "What do you mean?"

"I mean he knew from the moment we met that he was planning on using me for his bit of fun and then dumping me and he gave me a fake name thinking that meant he could just disappear and I would never find him or be able to make trouble for him," Sophie says.

"The bastard," I reply. "How do you know?"

"Well not long after I called you this morning, I decided to look at his Facebook profile and see if there was anything on there that should have made it obvious he was engaged and I just sort of chose to ignore it. I couldn't find the profile and I figured he'd blocked me right. So I logged in on my alternate account and looked him up that way. There are hundreds of Luke Fletchers, but none of them was my Luke. I was kind of annoyed but I was also curious. There was no way he knew about my alternative account to block that one as well and deleting the whole profile made no sense," Sophie said. "So I did a reverse image search of his profile picture on Google just to see if he had locked down the profile so tight it wouldn't show up in search results or anything. It led me to his real profile. Ugh you should see the pictures of him all loved up with his fiancé."

Sophie pauses for a moment. I'm still trying to process everything she's said so far. I really can't believe this guy has done this to her. The way she talked about him, he seemed so genuine. I realize Sophie is talking again.

"I'm seriously thinking about messaging her, you know. The fiancé. I mean doesn't she deserve to know what a prick she's marrying?" she says.

"Well yeah she does," I say. "But you realize he'll deny it and she's likely to believe him over you right?"

"Yeah, I know. Maybe I should just let it go. I might message him and just let him know that I know exactly who he is and to watch his back though. I'm not actually going to do anything to him, I just think it would be fun to worry him a bit. Or maybe it would be better to keep quiet so he doesn't block me from his real profile so I can keep an eye on things," she says.

"Honestly Soph, I think you should move on and forget about him. No winding him up, no stalking his profile. You deserve better than to have this cheating bastard taking up any space in your head," I tell her.

"Yeah, I guess you're right. But seriously if you could see the smug look on his face in his photos with her. It's like he's mocking her and she doesn't even know it. But I know. It's not my problem," Sophie says. "I'm going to send you the link to his profile though, just so you can see how smug he looks and tell me he doesn't deserve being brought down a peg or two."

"Ok," I say, curious to see what this guy is all about.

"Speak soon, I'll send it now," Sophie says and then she's gone.

I wait a second and my cell phone buzzes. It's Messenger and it's a message from Sophie of course. I open it and click the link she's sent me. My jaw drops when the profile opens. Yes, he looks smug in his profile picture, but that isn't what shocks me. What shocks me is his real name, Lewis Foley. I recognize his face instantly. Can this really be a coincidence that he not only sought out and dated my best friend behind his fiance's back, but also that he lied about his real name, almost as though he didn't want me to know he was dating Sophie.

Suddenly, I feel a deep dread gnawing away at my stomach. I remember Sophie saying she had told her boyfriend bits about Christian and me and how we were faking our relationship and how he had seemed so interested in the story. This is no coincidence. The bastard has been using Sophie to get information to use against Christian.

I storm across the lobby, typing out a response to Sophie about how yes, he does look smug in his picture and that we'll talk later because I'm going back into work. I could take a little bit longer to call her now and explain things – I know Christian wouldn't mind me being a minute or two late back from lunch – but I want to talk to him first and find out how much I can tell Sophie.

I wait impatiently for the elevator. It finally comes, I get in and I go up to our floor and hurry down the corridor to Christian's office. The more I think about it, the more annoyed I get and when I reach Christian's office, I'm so wound up I don't even bother to knock.

It's only once the door has banged off the wall where I pushed it open so hard that I realize Christian isn't alone in his office.

"I'm so sorry. I'll come back," I say, feeling the heat flood my cheeks.

"Stay."

It's not a request, it's a command and I realize with growing horror that it is Mr. Kramer talking. And then I see that the other man with him is none other than Lewis Foley. I feel a wash of anger flood over me. What I wouldn't give to claw his fucking eyes out.

"What's going on?" I ask, thinking I already know but hoping I'm wrong and the timing is just a coincidence.

"Sit down Ava," Mr. Kramer says and Christian jumps up and grabs me a chair.

I close the door and turn back to the room and Mr. Kramer looks at me with such disappointment that I just want the ground to open up and swallow me. This is exactly what I was afraid it was.

Christian smiles and gestures to the chair he's brought over. I sit down and he gives my shoulder a quick squeeze. I feel better for his touch. Whatever is happening here, however far into the argument they have gotten, Christian isn't mad at me and that's enough for me. Although I'm still sad that I've let Mr. Kramer down. Now that Christian and I have discussed our feelings for one another, I guess part of me envisioned us telling Mr. and Mrs. Kramer the truth about how we got together and all having a good laugh about it. But now someone else has gotten in first and told Mr. Kramer about it, it seems anything but funny. It seems like we were misleading him. Well we were, but this makes it feel cheap and sordid somehow.

"I'm very disappointed at how things have turned out here in my absence," Mr. Kramer starts, looking first at Christian and then at me.

Ok, maybe this isn't what I thought. Maybe we've messed something up with a client. It would still make sense for Lewis to be here if Mr. Kramer wants him to take over his half of the company instead of Christian.

"I expect this kind of nonsense from Christian, but not from you Ava. How could you lie to my face like that after everything I have done for you?" Mr. Kramer says, and any idea that this is about something other than Christian and me goes out of the window.

I debate playing dumb, but what's the point? He obviously knows and it will only insult him further if I try to lie my way back out of this. I don't know quite what to say, but it seems Mr. Kramer's question was a rhetorical question because he's talking again.

"I just... I don't know anymore. I thought you two had morals. What did he offer you to trick me Ava? Money? A place at the table? Come on. What's your price to betray me?" he says.

I wish he had made me answer the last question now because this one is even worse. I can feel shame flooding me and I don't know what to say. There's nothing I can say because he's right. I had a price tag and it was a price for betrayal. I force myself to look up.

"It wasn't as bad as you're making it sound. Christian wasn't ready to settle down and you were forcing him to do so in order for him to keep his inheritance. We weren't trying to betray you. We were trying to just not disappoint you," I say.

"Well I think it's fair to say you missed that mark," Lewis puts in. "You have both shown yourself to be morally corrupt and while it hurt me having to tell Jeff the truth and upset him, it was better than having you two continue laughing at him behind his back."

"No one was laughing at him," Christian puts in. He turns his focus to his father. "It's like Ava said. Sure I didn't want to lose my company to this bozo, but more than that, I didn't want to disappoint you and Mom."

Mr. Kramer opens his mouth to say something else, but quite frankly, I've had enough of being made to feel like shit. We made a stupid error of judgement, we got caught, and we know what Mr. Kramer thinks of us. But I'm not about to let Lewis be the hero here.

"How did you know?" I ask Lewis.

"Know what?" he says.

"That Christian and I had an arrangement rather than a relationship," I say. "How did you find out about that?"

"That doesn't matter," Mr. Kramer puts in.

"Maybe not to you, but it matters to me," I say. "Because if I'm going to be morally judged, it's not going to be by someone who cheated on his fiancé with my best friend and broke her heart along the way to get information to use against us."

Lewis instantly turns a beaming shade of red and Mr. Kramer glares at him.

"Is this true?" he demands.

"Yes, but I had my suspicions that Christian was up to something and then Ava came onto the scene and knew they were in it together. I had to get the evidence somehow," he says.

"And you decided the best way to do that was to fuck my best friend, make her fall for you and then break her heart?" I say. "And that's not to mention the fact you think it's ok to cheat on your fiancé."

"Ok, that's enough," Mr. Kramer says. "As much as I am not impressed with the way you got this information Lewis, this isn't about that. Lewis didn't lie to me. You two did. Now Ava, this is your chance to speak up. If Christian somehow coerced you into this or implied your job was dependent on it, now is the time to tell me."

"No. It was nothing like that," I say.

I saw a way to earn some easy money. A way that saved everyone's feelings. No one was meant to get hurt as a result of it. I don't say any of that though. I don't think Mr. Kramer wants to hear it. He's made his mind up about this. I could have lied and saved myself. Christian wouldn't have contradicted me. But I won't do that. We're in this together and if Mr. Kramer is going to hate him for this, then he can hate me too.

"Honestly Ava," Mr. Kramer says, shaking his head. "I just can't believe this. I know what you must be thinking. That Christian is my son, he should be getting the brunt of this, you were only an accomplice. But I just expected so much better from you Ava. I really did. Do you know when Lewis first told me about this, I laughed and told him there was no way you would do that to me?"

He keeps going on and the more he goes on, the more I want the ground to open up and swallow me. Nothing he is saying is wrong, but that doesn't make hearing it being said out loud by someone I have a massive respect for hurt any less.

CHRISTIAN

I suppose part of me expected this moment to come when I first asked Ava to be my fake girlfriend. But I thought it would come down the line, once the year was up and we all went back to normal. But then of course, I went and fell in love with Ava and nothing will ever be normal again. Once I realized that what Ava and I have actually could be real, things began to change, and then this morning, when she told me she loved me, I knew this would never be an issue. Either we would decide at some point to tell my parents the truth, or we wouldn't, but either way, there would be no fake break up and Ava and I would indeed settle down together.

It never even occurred to me that someone else might know about this. Especially not Lewis fucking Foley. If I had thought for a second he knew, I'd have been calling my father and telling him everything myself. See if Ava and I had told him first that what had started out as a lie had become something so real, he would have had no reason to disbelieve us. Now though, he will think it's more lies, just another way to continue on with this. I will lose the company. And it will be to the one person I really fucking hate in the world.

Except now I don't feel that hate quite so strongly. Maybe it's because now I have a much better outlet for my emotions. Maybe now that I have found love, I have no need for hate. I realize I shouldn't hate Lewis, I should pity him. Imagine being so pathetic that you run and tattle tale like this to get what you want.

I realize I've kind of tuned out of my father's lecture and I should probably listen because let's be honest, I deserve it. If I hadn't fallen for Ava, if she hadn't fallen for me, then we would be doing exactly what we're being accused of. But it's not really fair on Ava. While I didn't blackmail her to do this, it was all my idea and I did have to persuade her to go along with it. I knew what I was doing when I offered her so much money. I was dangling something that most people wouldn't be in a position to turn down.

I know that I've already lost the company and that hurts, but it doesn't hurt as much as the thought of losing Ava, and if I don't step in soon and stop my father from ripping her apart, then I'm going to lose her too. I'm not going to waste my time trying to convince my father that what I feel for Ava is real, but I do want her to know it.

I push my chair back and get to my feet. My dad stops talking and looks at me in surprise.

"That's enough," I say.

"Excuse me?" my dad says.

"You heard me. I said, that's enough. No one talks to the woman I love that way," I say. "And..."

My father interrupts me with a scoffing noise. I stop talking and raise an eyebrow at him.

"You can drop the act," he says.

"Funny you should say that. I dropped the act a week or two ago when I fell in love with Ava. And I know you're not going to believe that and quite frankly I don't care. You were right about the beginning though. I did coerce Ava into this. I made her an offer I knew she wouldn't be able to turn down because I was so intent on keeping this company. But then I began to see the real Ava and somewhere along the way, I fell in love with her for real," I say.

I turn my attention to Ava and I smile at her and she smiles back at me and it's like we're the only two people in the room, hell it's like we're the only two people in the world. And in some ways, I guess we are, because we are the only two people in the world that matter at this moment.

"Looking back now, it seems ridiculous the lengths I was willing to go to so that I could be the head of the company and gain my dad's approval. Now I can see that the company, while it is important to me, it's just a job. I can find another one easily enough. And my dad should be able to love me no matter what. I can walk away from the job and if my dad doesn't come around, I can walk away from him. But I can't walk away from you Ava. I love you more than all around the world and back again and now we're free," I say.

"What do you mean?" Ava asks me softly.

"Well Lewis is going to take over my job and I'm assuming you don't want to work for a snake like him so we're free to go anywhere and do anything. Together," I say.

"I like the sound of that," Ava smiles.

I think she gets me. I think she knows I'm choosing her over everything, but I need her to be certain that I am. Before I can change my mind, I get down on one knee and take one of Ava's hands in both of mine.

"Ava Long, will you do me the honor of being my wife?" I say.

"Christian you don't have to do this," Ava says. "I know what we have is real and if no one else wants to see that, then that's their problem."

I smile at her, loving her more in that minute than I ever have.

"This isn't quite as crazy as it seems. I'm not just doing it to make a point. I have an engagement ring in my car. I was planning on proposing at our weekend in Vegas, but this just seems right at this moment," I tell her.

Tears fill her eyes and she nods her head.

"Then yes, I would love to marry you," she says.

I get to my feet and pull Ava up and wrap her in my arms. Our lips find each other and as I kiss her, it occurs to me that I will never kiss a different set of lips and rather than scaring me, the thought makes me feel warm inside.

We come apart and spend a moment looking at each other until my dad interrupts the moment and reminds me that Ava and I aren't actually alone.

"Christian, Ava, I am so sorry," he says. "I... can you ever forgive me?"

I open my mouth to tell him I honestly don't know if I can. I could if it was only me he had a go at, but the way he went on at Ava was too much and I don't know if I can forgive that. I don't get a chance to say that though because Ava gets in first.

"Of course we can," she says. "We're in love now and our feelings are completely real, but in the beginning it was an act and you had every right to be pissed off about it."

My dad glances at me and I nod my head. If Ava can find it in her heart to forgive him, I can too, and I suppose looking at it the way Ava just said it, she's right, we did start out on a lie. My dad turns his attention to Lewis who hasn't spoken a word since Ava called him out on his own bullshit.

"Get out," my dad says.

"What?" Lewis says, clearly surprised that he is suddenly in the firing line.

"I said, get out. Are you deaf as well as stupid?" my dad fires at him.

"You can't talk to me like that. My dad still owns half of this firm and that half will go to me one day," Lewis says.

"Maybe it will and maybe it won't," my dad says. "But right now, you are nothing but a shit stirring little bastard who doesn't deserve a thing. You should consider yourself lucky that all I'm doing is dismissing you and not telling that fiancé of yours what you've been up to. But rest assured if I hear even a whisper of you so much as looking at another woman while you two are still together, I will tell her everything. Now get out before I change my mind and call her right now."

Lewis looks like he's ready to argue the point, but then he turns and storms out of my office, slamming the door behind him. I can't help but smile at his little rebellion and it seems my dad and Ava find it as funny as I do because after a second, the three of us are laughing until tears run down our cheeks.

When we've gotten ourselves under control a little bit, my dad smiles at me and then at Ava.

"Congratulations," he says.

"Thanks," Ava and I say together and that sets us off laughing again.

I've never known anyone who can make me laugh at something so trivial in a way that makes it seem like the funniest thing in the world, and even if we did kind of go around this the long way, I know this is the right outcome. Ava and I together could never be wrong.

"So obviously that little shit isn't getting his hands on any part of my half of the company," my dad says. "And if I get my way, he won't be getting his father's half either, but that's a battle for another day. Christian, Ava, I would very much like it if you stayed on in your current roles. I think the two of you together would be unstoppable."

I start to tell him I would like nothing more, but he raises a hand for silence so I stay silent and wait for him to continue.

"Before you reply, I'm being selfish, wanting you both to stay. Because what you said earlier about being free, that sounded pretty good to me, and if you two want to travel the world or do whatever you want to do and not be tied to the company, that's ok too. And you will both always be welcome to come back anytime. I realize that's a lot to think about, so I'm going to sneak off now and let you two have a talk about it. Just let me know what you decide. And either way, I'm happy for you both," he says.

He leaves the room and closes the door gently behind him. I look at Ava.

"Wow," I say. "I wasn't expecting that. What do you think?"

"I think right now I want you to kiss me and we'll worry about making this decision later," she says and I am more than happy to oblige her.

I kiss her and what starts out as a tender, loving kiss, soon becomes a hungry, passionate kiss. I'm trying to force myself to stop as my hands untuck Ava's blouse and roam over her bare skin, but it's like my mind and my body are acting separately from each other and I can't seem to make myself stop. I know I have no chance of stopping when Ava's hands grab my pants and undo my button and then my zipper.

She pushes one hand into my boxer shorts and the second she touches my cock I have to have her. I push her skirt up over her hips and lift her, carrying her towards the door. I rest her against the door so no one can walk in on us and then I push her panties to one side and run my fingers through her warm, wet lips.

It seems that Ava is as ready for this as I am, because she drops my cock and pushes my pants and boxer shorts down, and then she takes hold of my cock again, pulling me closer to her and lining me up with her pussy. I push into her, loving the warm, tightness of her. She's so slippery, so hot, and as I begin to thrust into her, I know neither of us are far from coming.

I slow down slightly, moving in and out of Ava in long, slow strokes. I kiss her mouth and then down her neck. The slow pace is only teasing me and judging by Ava's gasps and breathy plea of "please" I think I'm teasing her too. I give up any pretence of holding back and I begin to slam into Ava, hard and fast.

Her pussy tightens around me and she buries her face in my shoulder, her muffled voice saying my name over and over again as her body goes rigid and then soft again. She twitches, her muscles spasming in time with her pussy and the added tightness pushes me over the edge and I hit my orgasm.

Heat floods me, pleasure spreading through my cock and up into my stomach. I snatch a breath and hold it as the pleasure fills me, so intense it's almost painful yet so delicious I never want it to end.

I come hard, digging my fingers into Ava's hips as another wave of pleasure washes over me and then I slip out of her, sated, content and happier than I ever dreamed I could be. She unwraps her legs from my waist and stands down on the ground but she keeps her arms wrapped around my neck. I wrap my arms around her waist and for a long time, we just stand that way, holding each other like we never want to let go.

EPILOGUE

SIX MONTHS LATER

Ava

I lean back against Christian as he comes up behind me and wraps his arms around my waist. I put my arms over his, squeezing for a second and then relaxing as he kisses my shoulder. I'm still mesmerized, looking around the room and Christian does the same.

The walls are white with a border of yellow ducks. The floor is cream with a fluffy yellow rug. There's the light oak crib and the matching tiny wardrobe and set of drawers and my personal favorite thing, my rocking chair for those night feeds.

"It's beautiful isn't it?" Christian says.

I feel his breath tickle my neck as he talks. I nod my head.

"It is," I say. "I'm so glad we started with the nursery, but I wish the rest of the house was done."

"Be patient," Christian laughed. "It'll be done by the time Little Miss gets here."

"Oh you've decided we're having a girl have you?" I say with a smile.

"Yeah," Christian says. "And she's going to be a real daddy's girl."

He rubs his hand over my small bump and I feel a movement inside of me.

"See. Daddy's girl," Christian laughs when the baby kicks at his hand.

"Well she'd be crazy not to love you," I say. I turn in his arms and lean in and kiss him. "You're going to make an amazing father."

"And you are going to be the best mommy ever," Christian says.

I'm not so sure about that, but I am sure about Christian. We got married two weeks after he proposed to me, deciding we didn't want to wait. We had a small, intimate ceremony with only our close friends and family there and it was perfect. And Christian is an amazing husband. He always puts my needs before his. And that's how I know he will be an amazing father. Plus, it's clear how much he loves our baby already.

Christian

I can't believe Ava doesn't see what an amazing mom she's going to be. If I can be a quarter as good at being a parent as I know she's going to be, I will be happy. Not that I'm not happy now. I am. I'm one thousand percent happier than I have ever been.

I'm glad now that we decided against going off traveling. For a while, we truly considered it, but deep down, I think we both knew it wasn't really what we wanted. We told my dad the day after he made the offer, then we got married, Ava got pregnant on our honeymoon (or at least I like to think it was then. It could have been just before or just after it) and then we bought this house.

Traveling would have been fun, but it wouldn't have felt real. This feels real, like we are making a real commitment to each other and building a family, a life together. I love that feeling. And I love Ava. Every day I love her more.

I can't believe how lucky I am and I give Ava a squeeze and kiss her again. She kisses me back for a moment and then she pulls back slightly and smiles up at me. She steps out of my arms and takes my hand in hers and starts for the nursery door.

"Dinner?" I say, letting her lead me towards the door.

She shakes her head.

"No. I thought we could start on our bedroom," she says.

"Now?" I say, surprised. "Ava it's already after nine. You're pregnant and you're meant to be taking it easy."

"I know," she says all serious. She looks up at me and the seriousness gives way to a wide, playful smile. "But the bed isn't going to christen itself is it?"

"Ohh," I say as understanding dawns on me.

I don't need telling twice and I pick Ava up in my arms and run towards the bedroom with her, both of us laughing.

The End

Want to know when I have a new release?
Follow my Author Page:
https://www.amazon.com/Iona-Rose/e/B08LBNJQSD

Facebook Social Media: https://www.
facebook.com/IonaRoseAuthor/

ABOUT THE AUTHOR

Thank you so much for reading!
If you have enjoyed the book and would like to leave a
precious review for me, please kindly do so here:

Trouble With The CEO

Please click on the link below to receive info about my latest
releases and giveaways.
NEVER MISS A THING

Or
come and say hello here: